THE SEA IS CALLING...

# THE SIREN'S SONG

## SARAH ZANE

To everyone who has fought so hard to keep their heads above water just to find out they thrived underwater.

And to C for exemplifying so well what it means to be a bad ass woman who makes life bow to her that you snuck your way into this book.

# CONTENT WARNING

The Siren's Song is a story about a found family of ex nuns turned pirates who band together with the sirens of the sea to fight against a religious patriarchal society that has been trying to keep the women oppressed and kill the sirens. As a result, there are:

- mentions of genocide

- misogyny

- sexual abuse

- some violence and death

Please use your own discretion about whether or not the story is right for you.

# CHAPTER ONE
# Ray

From my first glance at my new roommate Coralina, I knew she was going to be a problem. My last roommate had recently moved out and I knew a new one was coming. I thought I was prepared, but I wasn't prepared for her. The gods had to be testing me because she was going to get me in trouble.

There was nothing about her blue eyes and long lashes, dark wavy hair, generous hips, or thick thighs that should have been dangerous, but they were a lethal combination to me.

*Seas claim me, she's beautiful*, I thought, knowing I couldn't be thinking like that.

When she greeted me with a hug instead of the expected handshake, I stiffened in her arms. I wasn't used to being touched and it took me a moment to relax enough to hug her back. She smelled of salt air and a hint of something sweet. I was half in love before I even pulled away from her hug.

I tried to keep her at arm's length for both of our safety, but my heart wasn't in it and she was stubbornly caring.

It wasn't her fault that I liked her more than I should, but it was too dangerous. Living in the Convent of the Saints of Santerra, the Saints' word was law. I knew their teachings well enough to know that they considered the feelings growing in me for Coralina to be blasphemous.

The list of blasphemous things a woman could do in the gods and the Saints' eyes was lengthy, but this was one of the most severe offenses.

Women were sinners by nature. The Saints taught us that only the love of a man could save us. If a woman loved another woman, she was embracing sin. I had lived in the Convent for long enough that I had met quite a few men who were far more sinful than any of the women I knew, but even if I didn't believe all the teachings of the Saints, it was hard to willingly defy the gods.

I wasn't ready for the risks, and if I really cared about Coralina, I wouldn't put her at risk, either. Women had to be careful. The Saints weren't all good men, but their teachings protected us from succumbing to the call of the sea. If a woman sinned enough, the gods would punish her, calling her to the sea and turning her into one of their monstrous sirens.

I tried to suppress my feelings, but Coralina's heart was even more beautiful than her face. I couldn't stay away from her, no matter how much I wanted to. I was too drawn to her, and I felt compelled to try to protect her. She was too kind for the Convent, and I was worried the less-than-holy Saints were going to ruin her. I had been living in this fortress they called the Convent for twenty of my twenty-five years, and meeting her felt like the gods were finally showing me the reason I was here.

She needed me. She was too kind to everyone, even to the Saints with the leering stares that the girls like me were smart enough to avoid. I wouldn't even meet the eyes of those lecherous Saints, never mind be kind to them. The Saints took what they wanted, so I was careful not to be desired.

It wasn't hard for me not to be wanted. I was never holy enough to be granted much time outside, so I was as pale as a ghost. My short, stringy blonde hair helped with the ghostly appearance, and thankfully, I didn't have the body the Saints preferred. Unlike Coralina with her full hips, thick thighs, and generous curves, I was too tall and stick-thin for them. I thanked the gods daily for that. My only remarkable feature was my green eyes. After hearing all my life that they were pretty and unique, I was careful not to meet anyone's eyes too often.

Coralina liked my eyes. She was the only one I didn't mind hearing that from. Mine were nothing compared to hers, though. Hers were the blue of the seas that I missed so much. I didn't have many memories from before the Convent, but I faintly remembered the smell of the salt air and splashing around in the sea with the sun shining down on me. That was the only real happy memory I had, and I longed for the sea like it was the home I didn't remember.

The Convent looked out on the water, but it was rare that I actually got to visit the water. The Saints said it was too dangerous for us because the call of the sea might overwhelm us, so they only let the holiest of us visit the surrounding towns and the sea. I was hardly ever chosen.

I was grateful we could see the water from the Convent at least, but it wasn't the same. I wanted to recapture that moment of joy of being by the water.

Being around Coralina felt the closest to that joy I had found yet. The blue of her eyes gave me that same feeling of warmth as my treasured memory.

I was doomed.

# Chapter Two
# Ray

Coralina was determined not to let me push her away and because of her stubbornness, we became fast friends. Before I knew it, she had gone from Coralina to Cora, and she started calling me Ray. I liked the sound of it. I had never felt much attachment to my actual name, Rayana. I had never been sure if the name was given to me by the Convent or by the parents who had sold me to them. It was possible that, like the home I couldn't remember, I once had another name.

Rayana didn't feel like me, but I liked the name Ray. Ray felt rebellious. Ray was a name I hadn't been assigned wasn't called by the Convent, and that in and of itself made me love it. That it came from Cora's lips made it even sweeter.

When I finally admitted to myself that I had fallen for her, I took solace in the fact that at least I wasn't putting her at risk. She didn't, couldn't, and wouldn't return my feelings, so I was only risking myself.

I prayed every night to the gods that they would take away my sinful thoughts, but as the days went by with the prayers unanswered, I started praying instead for forgiveness.

The Saints taught that the gods could read our thoughts and every night I feared that I would be called to the sea. I had been having blasphemous thoughts about the Saints for most of my life and now having feelings of attraction to Cora was sure to remove any remaining goodwill they had for me.

Contrary to my fears, every day I continued to wake up in our shared room and every day my attraction  and my fears grew. The gods didn't answer my prayers.

Worse still, Cora was becoming more attached to me. She insisted on staying by my side at meals, during worship, and even during chores when she could. She told the Saints she was trying to be a good influence on me, but a large part of me wondered if she was trying to protect me.

I had worried about her kindness making her a target, but I had underestimated her. Her kindness was her own form of protection. She befriended some of the better men in the Convent who kept the worse sort away from her. She was branded a nice girl who they would one day want to marry, not the sort to do sordid things with behind closed doors. Through skill or by luck, she was insulated from the worst of the Convent, and she seemed determined to extend that protection to me.

Her kindness may have helped save us from them, but it sealed our fates.

When she inevitably crossed the line, crossing our shared room to my bed and kissing me, I was already too in love to stop her.

I had so many conflicting feelings about it, but I wasn't strong enough to stop the best thing that had ever happened to me.

When she shared my bed that night and lay drifting off to sleep, my fears sank back in.

I imagined I was already hearing the sounds of the sea creep in, hearing the waves calling me to start the transition into the monster I truly was. Surprisingly, none of that happened. As the days went on, we got more and more comfortable.

We grew careless and stopped worrying so much about the gods and the consequences. Gods be damned, come hell or high water, she was worth it. But the threat of the Saints finding out became harder and harder to ignore.

# Chapter Three

# Ray

My joy managed to drown my fears for the short time before the Saints began to prepare for their latest sea cleansing mission. Every six months, they would pick a Convent woman they deemed holy enough and she would accompany them on a mission to fight against the evils of the sea. Their goal was to do the work of the gods and hunt the sirens plaguing the Isles of Santerra to extinction.

The hunting missions were normal and frequent, but a holy woman was only picked twice a year.

Normally, women were considered too much of a risk on the water. To be chosen was a high honor, and I was terrified that they were going to pick Cora this time. She was a favorite of many in the Convent, and the last thing I wanted was her sailing into that kind of danger.

I was worried about her, and about us. The girls that were chosen for the missions usually relocated shortly after, if they returned at all. Especially with our nightly sins, it was too dangerous for her. What if the sea called her while she was out there, and I never found out what happened to her? It was too much to bear.

When we both finished our duties for the night and made it back to our room, I begged her.

"Run away with me."

"What?" She laughed. "You can't be serious. I'm exhausted. It's too late for adventure."

"Cor, I'm serious. I can't lose you. They're gonna pick you."

She turned to me then and actually looked at me. I watched her blue eyes lose their mirth and shift to concern. She crossed the room to my side and took my hands in her own. She pulled me to the edge of my bed and sat with me. "You're serious, aren't you?"

"More serious than I've ever been about anything."

"I know you're worried, but I promise, you're not going to lose me. Nothing could keep me from you. Even if I go on their mission, it's only for a few days."

"Sometimes the women don't make it back."

She reached out and tucked a stray hair behind my ear and said, "I know you're worried, but I won't leave you. Maybe being picked could be a good thing. If I'm picked, it would mean we have the blessing of the gods, that they approve of us."

The hope on her face hurt to look at.

I couldn't meet her eye or match her growing smile. When she realized I wasn't coming around, her own smile faded. "It'll be okay, love, I promise. Good things are coming for us. I can sense it. Besides, we don't even know if I'll be picked."

I huffed out a sigh, aggravated. "Of course you will be. Everyone loves you. You're the most beautiful woman in the Convent."

She laughed at that. "You're such a flatterer, and it'll get you... everywhere." She smirked at me and more than anything, I wanted to be able to smile and laugh with her like usual, to be playful with her and kiss her, but I couldn't. This was too serious, and I was too scared.

"I'm sorry," I told her when I robbed her of her smile yet again. "I'm so sorry. I wish I could be as optimistic as you are, but I can't stop worrying. They're going to pick you. They always pick the holiest, most beautiful woman, and you're by far their favorite."

"They didn't pick me last time though," she pointed out.

"You'd only been here a few weeks last time."

It was hard to believe there had been a time not so long ago that I hadn't known her, and harder still to believe that there had been a time that I hadn't loved her.

"We should leave before they have the chance to take you from me," I tried again, knowing it was hopeless.

"But it's madness. We can't just leave. Where would we even go?"

"To your family? To another Isle? To the Zanarian mainland for all I care. We can't stay here."

She considered for a moment, letting go of one of my hands. Her hand seemed to move of its own accord and drifted up, starting to rub her locket. It was a nervous habit of hers and I suspected the necklace was a family heirloom.

I felt like a jerk for bringing up her family as soon as it left my mouth. You didn't get to the Convent by having a great family, but it was clear hers were rich. Maybe they just didn't know how bad things were here. Maybe they would be willing to help us for her sake.

It was unlikely, but I was desperate.

Her lips turned down into a frown. "We can't. You know we can't. We couldn't go far enough that the Saints wouldn't find us." I started to interject, but she stopped me, continuing, "We're marked. Even if we did make it out, we can't hide those forever. Someone would see and drag us back." Again, I started to interject, but a look from her silenced me. "And even if we could, we don't know what things are like off the Isle. It's possible the other Isles or the mainland are even worse."

"Unlikely," I said, unable to stop myself from interjecting.

"But not impossible," she countered. "Besides, we're in the service of the gods here. If we shirk our duties and leave the Isle, we would be called to the sea as penance. We wouldn't make it to the mainland if we left. The gods haven't forsaken us yet, but they certainly would if we abandoned the Convent."

"I would still go. If the seas called us or the hells themselves claimed us, I would go willingly to be with you."

"I love you with everything in me, you know that. But you can't ask that of me. I can't become a monster."

I understood her fears, but what she didn't understand was that I had lived here too long and seen too much. I had grown to fear the monsters in the Convent far more than the monsters in the sea.

I knew she wouldn't change her mind, so I stopped trying to convince her, but when the scrolls were read the next morning and she was picked, I couldn't help wishing I had tried harder.

She left that same afternoon. We were lucky enough to get a moment alone to say goodbye, but it wasn't nearly enough.

I pulled her into our room and the moment the door was shut, my lips were on hers. I needed her more than I needed air, but after a few short moments, she pulled away.

"We don't have enough time for that," she said, out of breath. "I'll be back in a few days, I promise."

I knew she would do everything she could to get back to me, but that didn't change that I didn't believe the gods would be that kind to me. I didn't believe I deserved her, and it was even harder to believe they would return her to me.

"Please trust me, I'll be back. I'll love you until the seas claim me."

Our little phrase hit harder now. She paused, waiting for my usual response, 'until the seas claim me,' but that didn't feel big enough anymore.

Instead, I said, "Until the seas claim me, and even after. You're my north star; I will always find you."

With one last kiss, she was smiling bright when she left. I managed to hold my composure until the door shut and then I let my tears fall.

# CHAPTER FOUR
## Ray

The week had been torture without her, and now that she was coming back today, I couldn't sleep. I tossed and turned until the first light started to creep in. It was no use. Sleep wasn't coming for me, so I gave up, got dressed, and made my way to my favorite place.

When I entered the chapel, a sense of calm enveloped me. I went over to the window bench I often claimed as my own and made myself comfortable.

It was my favorite, not because it was a little more comfortable than the rest, or because it would have been looking out at the sea if the window were transparent. I loved both of those things, but the real reason was the beautiful design on the colored glass window.

As I set to work on my sketching, the early morning light hit the colored glass just right, bathing the drawing in rainbow light.

I loved the effect and how it enhanced the beauty of whatever I was drawing. Not that the sketch of Cora I was working on needed any enhancing. Her beauty was breathtaking on its own but the colors helped my drawings come closer to mimicking her beauty.

I loved the quiet peacefulness of the chapel in the early morning. Most of the others didn't go to the chapels in their free time and this one was by far the least popular, making it my favorite in the Convent. With Cora away, our room felt too empty, so I had been spending a lot of time here over the past week.

I knew I didn't have much longer until I was called to work, but Cora was supposed to be home today and I wanted to have the sketch finished for her. I didn't have colors, so the black and white sketch couldn't capture the blue of her eyes or the sun-kissed glow of her skin, but I was determined to capture her as well as I could.

I wanted her to know that she had been missed, and working on the sketch helped me ignore my anxieties. I was doing this for her. The gods had to bring her back to me because I was spending all this time in the chapel sketching her. She needed to see it, so she had to come back.

As I worked, the light rose, changing the colors on the sketch from a calming blue and green to a raging orange and a lively yellow. The scene on the window was of a beautiful siren with a crown of seashells on her head and a vibrant green tail. It should have been eerie, since the sirens were violent and monstrous, but it was too beautiful for me to dislike. If the real sirens looked anything like this one, then I understood why men were so easily lured in by them.

I secretly thought that was the real reason the Saints were so determined to eliminate the sirens; they were easy prey for the beautiful creatures. The Saints claimed they were the saviors of the Isles of Santerra and that they were doing the work of the gods by slaughtering them, but it was hard to believe the gods would call for such brutality.

I had a harder time than most accepting that they were the monsters the Saints believed.

When the light on the sketch changed from yellow and orange to red, I knew I had to get going. I was due to start chores soon. I sighed and started to pack up my supplies, already dreading the day with Cora.

I was counting down the seconds until her return.

I had spent every waking moment she was gone praying to the gods that she would make it home safe, and now that the time was almost here, despite myself, I was starting to feel more hopeful.

I should have known that the gods would punish me. They let my negative thoughts about the Saints slide. They even let my relationship with Cora slide, but now they were punishing me for my worst sin of all, hoping. I had dared to hope for a better life, for a better future with her. Cora was my everything, and that devotion was a sin for which she and I paid dearly.

# CHAPTER FIVE
## Ray

She didn't come back with the ship.

She didn't come back at all.

She was called to the sea, and it was all my fault.

# CHAPTER SIX
# Ray

The rest of the Convent gave me a wide berth in the days after.

I didn't know if they suspected the truth of what Cora had been to me, or if they just didn't want to be pulled down by my grief, but they left me alone.

Alone with my thoughts to mourn and wonder what the hell had really happened to Cora.

The more I thought about it, the less it made sense.

The Saints said she had been called to the sea for her sins, but if that were true, why had she survived so long here with me?

She wasn't called to the sea on any of the nights she spent in my arms. Then, as soon as she went on a holy mission with the Saints, she disappeared. I was supposed to believe it was because of her sins? It wasn't adding up.

It wasn't unbelievable for a Convent woman to get called to the sea, but it didn't happen often. Girls and women from the surrounding villages and other isles got called much more frequently. At the Convent, we were supposed to be more protected. The Saints taught us to be holy and defended us from the call of the sea, the call to sin. It wasn't unimaginable that someone from the Convent could be lost to the seas, but it was unbelievable that it was her.

Cora was the kindest woman I knew. Most of the girls sent to the Convent were troublemakers sent to the Saints to teach them to live a holy life. They paid the families of the surrendered children well, rewarding their sacrifice for helping rid the seas of one more siren.

I was paid for, Cora wasn't.

Cora had come here of her own volition to be a good influence on us all. It wasn't uncommon for a holy volunteer to live with the sinners at the Convent. Cora wasn't the first and wouldn't be the last woman the Convent took in for that purpose, but even among the holy chosen ones, she was a favorite of theirs. I couldn't blame them though. She had an incredibly big heart and had come here because she believed in the mission of helping better the Isles.

There weren't many women in the Isles who would sacrifice their freedom to help us lost sinners.

Cora had.

In her place, I doubted I would've done the same.

It was one of the many reasons Cora was often sent out to preach the word of the Saints and bring food to the surrounding villages.

This was a recent development. The Saints had proclaimed that since many of the sinners of the Isle were coming to the light, the gods saw fit to bless our villages. Had they done that back when I was a child, I might never have come to the Convent in the first place.

I hadn't been alive in what the Isles referred to as the pre-salvation times, but I knew the Saints hadn't always ruled the Isles. They said they came to save us from the sirens plaguing our waters and the sins plaguing our hearts.

It seemed like I was the only one that saw that instead of nourishing our Isles, they instilled fear in us all.

I was five when they bought me and hadn't known a moment of peace since then, until Cora. The Saints brought us up fearing ourselves. I was constantly reminded of the danger that I was in, that at any moment I could be called to the sea and turned into a siren, cursed to live out the rest of my life as a monster until the Saints found and mercifully ended my life.

That's what they called their mission to eradicate the sirens, mercy killings for sinners, saving their souls.

The truth behind the façade was that everything the Saints did was calculated.

They liked to hide the truth of their cruelty as much as they could, but I knew the Saints better than that. As much as they tried to convince me otherwise, I wasn't here because I was a sinner; I was here because the Convent paid well for girls when none were willingly sent. The parents I no longer remembered had sold me to the Convent, telling me it was the only way they could give me a better life.

Even then, I could sense the lie.

When the gold changed hands and I was taken to the dark, dingy Convent and given chores, no longer allowed to play or have a carefree childhood, I knew I wasn't the one who had been given a better life.

I wondered if my former parents still believed the lie they told themselves, that they had saved me.

They hadn't saved me. The Saints hadn't saved me. Even the gods hadn't saved me. If anyone had saved me, it was Cora. She showed me my first touch of kindness, my first taste of love. Now I was supposed to believe that that same bright, beautiful girl had been stolen by the sea, by the gods' will?

It didn't make any sense.

Even in my worst nightmares, where the gods did punish us, we were punished together. I would have willingly gone to the sea with her or to the worst of the hells if I could just keep holding her hand. The thought that she was suffering without me was unbearable. The thought that I had lost her, that I was somehow spared, and she wasn't, was irreconcilable. She was my better half. If the gods couldn't see that, then damn them and their judgment.

That the gods would punish her when they could have punished me instead was unfathomable. It couldn't possibly be true. I had been a sinner in my thoughts long before she came along. If they wanted to punish someone, it should have been me.

If they had punished me, it might have scared Cora back to what they considered to be the right path, but they hadn't. They had punished her, and without her, I was about to get so much worse.

If what the Saints said was true and she was claimed by the sea, out there swimming right now as a siren, I would find my way back to her. By sin or by sail, I would find her. If she couldn't be saved, I would join her, but on my life, I would find her.

If it wasn't true and the Saints had done something to her, the gods were going to need a stronger word than sin for the atrocities I would commit to the men that hurt her.

#  Chapter Seven
## Coral

I didn't recall much of my life from before my transformation day. Despite how hard I tried, I couldn't remember anything from before I heard the call of the sea and was claimed by the waves.

My transformation day was all that lingered in my memory. Those final hours were burned into my mind, and into the siren's.

The siren remembered and called for blood—for *their* blood. The siren yearned to attack every ship that passed, to bring it to the bottom of the ocean in case one of the men responsible for my transformation was onboard. Every time a ship passed, I had to yank hard on the siren's leash, trying to fight her urges.

I knew the siren and I were one and the same, but it was hard to think of the siren as myself. The siren felt foreign to me, like a state of mind that took over when I couldn't fight my new instincts. I imagined my sisters had all faced the same internal struggle, but they were well enough adjusted now that it was hard to picture.

I was the newest of the pod, my sisters all having surrendered their humanity long ago. Their eyes were wild and their teeth were sharp when they grinned. They were almost animalistic. I knew I must look like that too, but the remaining surface-dweller part of me was scared of them.

They weren't cruel to me, though. They cared for me, had saved me, but it was hard to ignore the joy they took in drowning and torturing men. It was hard to digest the glee the siren took in it, that *I* took in it.

With every new ship that passed, the urges grew stronger, and I had to try my best to suppress them. As hard as I tried, I was still learning. The siren screamed for blood and sometimes I couldn't stop her. Sometimes, I didn't even bother trying. My sisters understood. They all dealt with the same urges. If my siren attacked, they would follow. No siren was left behind; if one fought, we all fought.

But it was dangerous. The hunters didn't mess around. They had their weapons against us, and sometimes one of us wouldn't make it. Sometimes, they would use nets. We took extra pleasure in killing those who tried to capture us. We all knew the risks, and we all knew we would rather die than be captured.

Word had spread through the ocean about a siren who had been captured and had unspeakable things done to her. By the time I came to the pod, it was common knowledge that death was preferable, so we took precautions. We all wore poisonous seaweed around our wrists, harmless to the touch but toxic when eaten. My pod had lost a few sisters that way when they couldn't free themselves from the nets in time.

It was a steep price, so my pod tried to keep to ourselves and out of trouble. I tried to keep a leash on the siren's urges, and luckily the others seemed adept at doing the same. As a result, we usually avoided the hunters, but it seemed like lately there were more ships about, and most carried hunters.

It was becoming impossible to avoid them. As hard as my sisters and I fought our urges, with hunters as close as they were, we were attacking more than was safe.

My siren was growing angrier with each passing day, and harder to control. Even when we attacked the ships, it wasn't enough. The blood didn't sate her for long. I was starting to suspect it wouldn't until the blood belonged to one of the men from my transformation day.

I remembered every moment of the day those men used me for their ritual. I was sure I would recognize the faces of almost every man who had touched me.

I could never forget their rough hands shoving me down as they took turns doing whatever they wanted to me. I was terrified and in pain, screaming, but still they didn't stop. They just shoved a dirty rag into my mouth to stop my screams. They didn't silence me out of fear of discovery, but simply because my screaming annoyed them. They laughed about it and said it was a pity they weren't going to be keeping my pretty mouth available. I thought maybe then they would stop, but they didn't. There were still more that wanted their turn.

My memories of my surface days started and ended with the pain on that ship. I couldn't remember what the ritual they were doing was or why I was there in the first place, but if that's how surface dwellers were, it was better that the waves had claimed me.

Even with the rag in my mouth, I still screamed my lungs out, but they hadn't cared or stopped. I prayed to anything that was listening that it would stop, but it didn't. Only when I was so badly hurt that I was wishing for death did it stop.

The hands finally let go.

I was thankful, for a moment. I'll never forget how I breathed out in relief, until the hands were replaced with rough ropes around my arms, binding them behind my back. I was too tired to fight much, but I pushed back against the men with everything I had left. I pulled against the ropes with all my strength, but it was no use.

I flailed, kicking with my legs, but they were swiftly bound until I couldn't move an inch. The ropes burned against my bare skin. Any of the skin unmarred from their advances had been rubbed raw by my attempting to get out of the ropes.

Two of the men hoisted me up, and I prayed whatever happened next would end my life quickly. It wasn't until I felt the fresh air on my skin that I realized what they intended, and I felt the tears come.

Those waters were infested with sharks. I hoped I would drown quickly and just slip away peacefully beneath the waves, but if I didn't, I hoped that sharks would get me before the sirens did. At least the sharks would make it quick.

Falling into the hands of the sirens was a far worse fate than being found by sharks. But I would have taken either instead of staying on the ship with those monsters. If given the choice, I would have picked the sea every time. There wasn't a fate worse than what had already happened to me.

The men tied something heavy to my feet, dashing my last slim hope of escape. They were still laughing when they tossed me overboard. The hard slap of the ocean against my legs stung almost as much as the salt water on my wounds. My entire body was on fire as the water closed in around me, silencing the world.

I opened my eyes. The salt stung and all I could see was blue. I tried to push the rag out of my mouth with my tongue, but that only hastened the water entering my mouth, so I stopped.

I tried tugging on the rope around my wrists, but it wasn't any use. The weight continued to drag me down as I watched the surface slowly grow farther and farther away. I wasn't going to survive this. I tried to make my peace with the end, until a moment later when I saw the flick of a tail out of the corner of my eye.

I tried to thrash when I felt a fin brush my back, but I was too wrapped up to move my body much.

*Please be a shark, please be a shark.*

A moment later, my worst nightmare floated into view. It wasn't a shark.

The siren had a long grey tail like a shark. She had piercing eyes and white flowing hair, but I knew better than to be taken in by her beauty.

She moved closer, and I flinched.

She grinned at that and her sharp teeth made me scream. Water rushed in through the little space around the rag in my mouth. Panic overtook me, until a thought that felt foreign broke through the haze of terror.

*Hush, little one. Death has you in its clutches, but there's another way.*

I felt my vision going hazy as I clung to life as hard as I could.

*Tell me, little one, do you want to live?*

I was either hallucinating the siren or the voice in my head or both, but I still considered the question, and with my last remaining moment, realized I did. I wanted to live.

The world went black, and when my senses slowly returned, there was something warm pressed against my lips. If this was death, maybe I was wrong about wanting to live.

The warmth pulled back, and I opened my eyes to find I was staring at the grey-tailed siren. She had just had her lips on mine. I gasped and touched my lips with my fingers. This couldn't be real. I quickly realized a few impossible things: I didn't appear to be dead, I wasn't choking on the water, I didn't have the rag in my mouth anymore, and my hands were free.

*I don't understand.*

A melodic laugh flowed through my mind followed by the thought, *Of course not, little one. It's quite common to be confused on your transformation day.*

I blinked and looked at the siren.

*That was your voice!*

She nodded. *Ah—a bright one. I do hope that will make this easier for you.*

I didn't know where to begin or what to think or ask.

*Why am I not dead?*

*Would you rather be?* the voice of the siren asked in my mind. I could hear the curiosity in her words.

*No, I suppose not,* I thought automatically. *But what now? And how am I still here?*

*Now, we welcome you into the pod. It's been a while since we've added a sister. The others will want to meet you right away.*

*But...but...I can't join you.*

*And why not?*

*Because I should be dead? Because I don't belong here? Because none of this should be possible?* A million answers rushed through my mind before I settled on the most obvious one. *I'm not a siren. If you would just unbind my legs, I can make my way back to the surface and won't have to burden you.* I hoped my thoughts were convincing.

She just blinked slowly, looking down at my legs and then meeting my eye.

*I'm afraid I can't do that.*

I knew this was a trap. I knew it—or I should have known, anyway.

Some of that must have shown on my face, because she shook her head. *You're not understanding, little one, look down.*

I did and couldn't comprehend what I was seeing. Where the brown ropes had been was a mass of violet. I tried to move my legs under it by kicking my feet and screamed in surprise when a tail flicked out where my feet should have been.

*I'm—I'm—* I couldn't even finish the thought. *But that's impossible!*

*You wanted to live, and my sisters and I try to save those we can, but you were too far gone to be saved. A choice between living under the waves or dying under them was all I could offer you. I'm sorry that I didn't find you sooner.*

I tried to understand, but I was slow in taking in the reality of my situation. I had lived above the waves all my life. I was sure of that. I wanted to get back to the surface, wanted to fight for my life above the waves.

I was sure there were memories of that life somewhere in my mind, but I couldn't think, couldn't understand what I had been fighting for. All I could remember was the pain those men had put me through. If that was all the surface had to offer, I was better off below the waves.

I let the siren take my hand and lead me into my new life.

The grey-tailed siren, who I later found out was Charia, brought me into her pod. Just like she said, the rest of my new sisters were just as welcoming as she was.

I tried to leave the nightmare of my surface life behind, but the memories of my fear and pain were still visceral, and the siren clung to them. I kept wishing the siren inside would forget so I could, too, but the memories weren't going anywhere.

I wasn't the only one still plagued by the horrors that brought me here, and there was comfort in that shared pain.

Every one of my sisters had a story just as gruesome. Rezi, one of my siren sisters, had been found with wounds that took months to heal. When she refused her ship's captain because she preferred the company of women, they had beaten her and driven nails through the flesh of both of her hands and fastened her to the front of the ship. They said if she loved women so much, she would make good siren bait.

They were right.

The moment my siren sisters sensed her fear, the men didn't stand a chance. The ship had been brought down swiftly, and Rezi was adopted into the pod. I hadn't yet succumbed to my fate, so I hadn't witnessed the monstrosity, but the still-visible scars on her hands were reminder enough of the dangers of the surface and the men who hunted us.

My only regret was that my sisters hadn't been around when Charia found me, so the ship got away. It wasn't often a ship made it away from our pod unscathed, so they could count themselves lucky, until I found them again.

# Chapter Eight

# Ray

The truth was easier to uncover than I expected. I had unknowingly trained my whole life for this. The Convent had taught me the important lesson of how to disappear into the background and be forgettable. I learned early on it was the easiest way to avoid punishment. I didn't care about being liked or winning favor, just about avoiding punishment. Being forgotten was the easiest path, and the skill served me well now.

It was easy to overhear conversations when people forgot you were there.

Of course, I asked around about Cora first, but the other girls continued to ignore me, or worse, pity me. They believed what they were told, that Cora had been called to the sea, and that I was delusional in looking for more meaning behind it. They knew I was grieving the loss of my best friend and instead of being compassionate, they told me that if I didn't start shaping up, I would be next.

If only it were that easy to follow in her footsteps. I would be gone already.

I started taking extra cleaning shifts, trying to keep my mind off things and stay out of my room, but also to get closer to certain Saints. Someone was bound to know something. Plenty of them had considered Cora a friend, but asking around wasn't getting me far at all. All of her so-called friends clammed up at the mention of her and wouldn't talk to me about her. They said it was unwise to talk about sinners and tempt the gods to call another.

It was a weak excuse, but I knew I wasn't going to get anything out of them, so I kept my head down and kept working. I knew they would get careless, eventually. When it came to Cora, I could be patient, and sooner or later, someone would let something slip.

A week later, I was sweeping the halls when an unfamiliar Saint stalked by. I had lived in the Convent nearly my whole life, so it was unusual to see a stranger, and I was sure I would have remembered this man. He was tall and willowy with scraggly facial hair and a permanent sneer. He was walking next to one of Cora's friends, Garrick.

I liked Garrick. He was always nice enough to me and he was sweet on Cora in a hopeless but adorable way. He doted on her, never understanding that she didn't see his kindness as anything more.

Maybe I should have felt jealous, but he was sweet, and I liked that was kind to her. Even if he did have an ulterior motive, she liked being around him, so I liked him.

I wasn't sure what he was doing meeting with a stranger though. He wasn't one of the higher ones so him having a solo meeting with a stranger was unusual, and Garrick looked nervous.

I kept my head down as they walked past, continuing to sweep as they took a right and stepped into an office.

I slowly crept closer, curiosity getting the best of me. I was encouraged to see they hadn't fully shut the door. I sidled up close to the gap and held my breath, hoping I didn't get caught and that if I did, whatever I was about to hear was worth the risk.

"Has that pesky girl finally stopped asking questions?" the newcomer demanded.

Garrick nodded quickly. "Yessir, she and Coralina were close, but she's finally stopped asking after the girl."

*Coralina!* I thought with a start. *So I was right. This was important. If this was about Coralina, I had to be the pesky girl they were complaining about. Well,* I thought with no small amount of satisfaction, *at least I'm inconveniencing them.*

"Good. If she didn't stop, she would've had to be next, and the gods know we wouldn't have enjoyed that."

They both laughed at that while I stared at them in disbelief. I wasn't sure I entirely understood the threat, but it was clear that's exactly what it was. If I didn't stop asking around, they were going to do to me what they did to Cora. They had done something to Cora. If they took me, I wouldn't be able to help Cora if she was still able to saved.

Whatever I did, I was going to have to be smart about it until I found out what really happened to her. If there was any hope for Cora, I needed to be around to help her.

"She won't be a problem," Garrick said. "She was just obsessed with Coralina. It'll pass."

I was so upset by his words that I almost missed his gesture. He was rubbing a silver locket between his finger and thumb, and I just barely managed to stifle my gasp. The gesture was hers, and without having to be any closer to it, I knew it in my heart that the locket was hers too.

She never took it off. Even when we lay in bed together without anything else on, the necklace had always stayed.

If the sea had called her, she would have had her necklace. Whatever had happened to her hadn't been natural. They had done something to her, something terrible, and the man standing in front of me wearing her necklace was going to die by my hand. If it was the last thing I did, I was going to slit his throat and take back her necklace.

"It's a shame we couldn't have taken more time with Coralina, though. She was my favorite," Garrick said, still caressing her necklace. It took everything in me to not burst in there and strangle the life from him right then and there.

"An unfortunate side effect of the ritual. The sirens get restless. We had other priorities, but you all did well. Keep up the good work and you'll be on the next cleansing mission."

"Yessir, thank you, sir."

They both headed toward the door, and I quickly scampered around another hallway and resumed my sweeping, praying they weren't coming this way. They hadn't noticed me the first time, but I didn't think I could avoid their notice a second time, and I knew I couldn't speak to either of them right now. I wasn't sure what I would do if either of them approached me, but it wouldn't be smart. I was too angry to hide my emotions.

Before their footsteps had faded, I had the beginnings of a plan.

# Chapter Nine

## Coral

I felt the vibrations in the water before I heard or saw any sign of the incoming ship. The ocean itself was vibrating, warning us, whispering, *A ship is coming.*

*Here we go again.*

I had lost track of time, but several lunar cycles had passed since my transformation, and we had taken down more than a few ships, but I already knew this one would be different.

Even the vibrations of the water felt different this time. The waves themselves seemed to know something big was coming. My siren was already yanking at the tight leash I kept her on. The instincts came too soon, too hard. I had thought I was ready to fight her off, but I wasn't ready for her intensity. She knew this felt different, too. I tried to hold her back, but it was useless, so I let go.

She took over. I was only watching through her eyes. I couldn't control a thing. I wished I could look away, but I couldn't. The surface-dweller in me hated this part. I took no pleasure in the animalistic, bloodthirsty way she took down ships and murdered men, but I had no choice but to watch.

With her enhanced senses, I noticed what I hadn't before; the ship coming toward us looked familiar, but more importantly, she had already heard the cries for help. Feminine cries, followed by male laughter. She turned to my sisters and, from the grins on their faces, I knew we were all feeling the same. The ocean was going to run red with their blood.

I sent the thought to my sisters, more of a warning than a request, but they nodded. I was taking the lead on this. They would follow.

Ostoma and Rezi would be ready to tend to the women if they were joining us, or to help them to safety if they weren't. The other three followed closely behind my siren.

I swam up to the boat and...

*THWACK!*

My siren slammed my violet tail against the bottom of the ship.

With sharp-toothed grins, my sisters set to work doing the same. The ship was smaller than the hunter's ships we were used to.

*THWACK!*

*THWACK!*

*THWACK!*

My siren's tail and my sisters' tails continued to beat against the hull until we heard male screams. I couldn't see the men, but I could hear their panic and almost taste their fear as we launched the ship sideways.

*THWACK!*

*THWACK!*

*THWACK!*

We kept at it until finally the hull gave way, our tails puncturing holes in the bottom of the ship. I grinned at my sisters and signaled. I took the lead with Lucia and Sypher behind and Charia bringing up the rear. In formation, we were fast, precise, and deadly.

We moved away from the ship, weaving as we did in case of a counterattack, but none came. There were only panicked cries of scared men. I reveled in their fear. I was going to put those low-life surface-dwelling scum into a watery grave.

The ship started to sink lower as it filled with water. They rushed to their lifeboats and piled in. When we saw that the distressed women who had caught our attention were being left on the ship, I knew my siren had made the right decision. The despicable hunters weren't even trying to save the women.

Ostoma and Rezi were under the ship now, waiting for their opportunity to rescue the women, leaving the fun part to the rest of us.

We watched from a short distance as the rowboats hit the water. Sometimes, my sisters would untie the lifeboats, taking away all hope of escape from the men, but when I was in charge, I always kept them there. Lifeboats or not, they wouldn't escape us, and it was delicious watching their hopes be dashed when they saw us. Delicious knowing they had tasted escape before we tasted their blood.

As the lifeboats started to move, I felt a tug toward the one on the left.

*That one is mine,* I thought and then flicked over to it, staying under the water, out of sight. There were four other boats that the others doled them out among themselves. It hardly mattered—this one was mine.

The men all rowed hard, but in the wrong direction. The shore was close by if they turned around, but they kept going the wrong way. I launched myself far enough away to safely surface and popped my head out of the water, just enough so I could see, and looked around.

The air was thick with fog. The fog was no match for my siren eyesight, but it wasn't hard to imagine that the surface dwellers likely couldn't see the land they were rowing away from. They didn't seem to be able to sense it, either. They were a sorry excuse for seamen. Even if we weren't here, who knows how long they would have survived.

I resubmerged and waited for them to get a little closer. When they were halfway to me, I surfaced again. This time, I pushed my head fully above water, and the siren began her call.

The song was always the same, a lament to lost love, full of sorrow but promise, promise that things could be better if only they would get into the water, if only they would listen and surrender themselves to me, to us. We could make all their problems go away.

My sisters joined in the song, taking up their positions near the other lifeboats.

I crept closer, I felt the waves respond to me, felt my song calling out to the men. I heard the men's hearts quicken a moment when they sensed the danger, sensed me. Then I had them enthralled and their hearts slowed. There were only fifty of them, ten in each boat. A smaller crew than normal, but there would be enough to go around. My sisters could have the rest. I only wanted him. This lifeboat had called to me because of him. I remembered enough to know he was one of the men who held me down on my transformation day. He had held me down and shoved the dirty rag in my mouth.

Tonight, I would have my revenge. Tonight, I was the hunter, and he was going to pay.

Before I made it within a hundred feet of his boat, I heard a splash. I almost broke my song to laugh. That must be a new record. Normally, the men held out much longer, trying to resist. I felt the water move around the man, felt the vibrations of one of my sisters coming from below. She pulled him under. The moment the water filled his ears, the spell was broken.

I felt his screams vibrate through the water and the laugh of my sister as she bit into him. So it was that kind of night. I grinned through my song, ripe with anticipation.

We didn't eat the men. We weren't monsters, we just exacted revenge. The worse the condition of the women we rescued, the slower the deaths we gave the men. This man had put me through hell, and he was going to die screaming, alone yet surrounded, and afraid, like he and his friends had intended for me.

I was within fifty feet of him now. A few more went overboard and were quickly dragged under. Then there were five. It seemed my prey was one of the stronger-willed. Good. The stronger the will, the more pleasurable it would be to break. I would take my time with him.

The men could see me now, slowly emerging from the fog. The very image of their desires, the answer to their darkest prayers. *Come to me,* I sang just for him, and he did. The others jumped into the water, too, following close behind, but he was the quickest. I watched as he closed the distance between us, letting him come to me. It was sweeter that way, making him chase his own doom.

I signaled with a flick of my tail in his direction, claiming him. I knew my sisters were lurking about. I didn't care about the other men. They would only get in my way, but *he* was mine.

I felt the other men be pulled under the water. Perfect timing. He finally closed the distance and wrapped his arms around me. I wrapped mine around him and dug my sharp nails into his back. He was so far under my spell that he didn't even flinch at the blood emerging from the wounds.

Then, only then, seeing the lust and devotion in his eyes, holding him tightly in my arms, did I stop singing.

I watched his eyes, watched the dawning realization that I wasn't whatever fantasy his mind had come up with. I watched as he took in my face and brushed up against his leg with the end of my tail. I felt his heart speed up and saw his pupils dilate. His muscles tensed, and I knew he was right where I wanted him.

Right before he tried to pull away, I grinned, letting him see my razor-sharp teeth. He screamed as I pulled him under.

My sisters and I slept well that night. We always did after such an active night.

Well, most of us did.

Ostoma and Rezi stayed up tending to the new recruit, whom they had saved just in time. The other women had been alive enough to be brought to shore, but this new one had been unsavable. Even now, in siren form, she was only alive thanks to Ostoma's healing. I knew it would be far from an easy night for her. The first was always the hardest, but she was in good hands. And more importantly, the other hands that had touched her were food for the sharks now.

I rested easy knowing those particular hunters would never touch anyone else ever again.

# Chapter Ten
# Ray

I stopped sketching in my free time and poured all my non-working hours into training. I was strong for a woman, but that wasn't going to be enough if I was really going to kill Garrick.

And I was.

I didn't have a choice; he needed to die.

He had her locket. The one I had never once seen her without. She wouldn't ever have willingly parted with it. She would have taken it to the grave with her if given the choice.

The fact that he had it meant I couldn't avoid the truth; she was dead.

Whatever the Saints had done to her before that, he had been a part of it. He was her *friend,* or so she thought, so he needed to die.

To make that happen, I needed to be stronger. I knew I wouldn't get away with it. There would be no hiding his death or hiding from the consequences. I would be killed for it, but at least I would be with her.

I could do this. I could be strong one last time for her.

I was competent at self-defense, but I knew I would need more than a little luck to pull off what I was planning. I was going to force Garrick to tell me what they did to her, and then I was going to kill him and take back her necklace. If she couldn't die in it, I could at least honor her by taking it to my own grave.

I stayed up most nights for a week, sleeping an hour or two when I could spare it, but most of my time I spent practicing my fighting skills. Using a broom and a kitchen knife, I spent hours fighting my pillow opponent. It wasn't much, but it was the best I could do to prepare. Sparring kept the rage in me from boiling over.

I was impatient, but knew I had to wait a little longer. I had to strike when the time was right.

Soon the crew for the next hunt were going to be announced. If Garrick was going to be on the ship, I would have to act fast. If I pulled it off, no one would know he was missing until the ship returned without him. I would try to hide his body and his death as long as I could. I knew she would want me to survive, but even as I meticulously planned this, I didn't think it would work. I highly doubted I would survive much longer than he would.

# CHAPTER ELEVEN
# Ray

Garrick was picked for the next hunt, giving me just under a week to make my move. I decided to try on the fifth day, giving myself a chance to start again if the first attempt wasn't successful. After all, I didn't know where Garrick would be most of the day. In order for my plan to work, I would need every ounce of luck I could get.

By a stroke of luck–or misfortune depending on perspective–a couple days before I planned to strike, I got a new roommate.

Her mere presence rubbed salt in my already raw wounds. It had hardly been long enough to replace Cora. I hated the Saints even more for that. The rest of the Convent had already moved on and were pretending she didn't exist. Our room was the only place I could still feel her, and now they were taking that away, too.

I shouldn't have been surprised at their cruelty. If anything, it was surprising they waited this long.

I was determined to hate the new girl on principle, but I couldn't even do that right.

The new woman, Scyla, felt like a kindred spirit, and she seemed even more out of place here than I was.

Her dark brown skin and locs weren't typical of our part of the Isles. I wondered if that meant the Saints were extending their reach, pulling women from the smaller Isles to the Convent on Santerra proper.

I had hoped things might have been better for the Santerrans who didn't live on Santerra proper right under the thumb of the Saints, but apparently not if Scyla's presence was anything to go by.

It wasn't her skin or her hair that really made her look out of place though. It was that she had the look of a laborer. With her strong biceps and sculpted legs, she looked more fit for the seas than for the Convent. Her body was an impressive feat managing to balance out her muscle with a generous chest and sculpted ass I felt guilty looking at.

*Not that Cora would have cared. Hells she would've been looking with me.* That thought was the first time since Cora left that I had smiled.

Scyla recognized right away that I was going through something horrible and made it her mission that night to make me laugh. By the end of the night she had more than succeeded and I resigned myself to calling her my friend.

Which was unfortunate, because it meant I cared and would worry about her. It wouldn't matter so much if she didn't stick out as much as she did. Even if she wasn't as stunning as she was, she was going to be too much of a target at the Convent.

She carried herself with too much pride. The Saints wouldn't put up with that for long. Gods, this place would beat the spirit out of her soon if she wasn't careful. She would have to learn quickly to walk with her head down and blend in. If she didn't, the men would give her more attention than was safe, or worse, might see fit to teach her a lesson, to punish her for some invented sin.

That first morning, I tried to warn her, but she just grinned at me like she knew a secret I didn't. There was something in her eyes that made me almost believe that she would be okay, but that something felt too dangerously close to hope.

Hope was insidious and dangerous. It snuck its claws into you when you least expected it and twisted your logic. It made you believe good things would happen before sticking you with the worst heartbreaks.

Hope had a steep price that I couldn't afford to pay.

My hope had killed Cora, and I refused to let any of it back in.

It was clear Scyla still had hope, clear that she was determined not to let this place break her.

Miraculously, she made it back to our room that night in one piece. I thought for sure she would have been dragged away for punishment or someone's pleasure, but she was back.

She shut the door behind her with a sigh. Reaching into the folds of her robe, she pulled out a piece of rolled up parchment and tossed it on her bed.

I was going to ask about it, but before I could, she started to pull off the robe.

I knew I should look away, the gods knew I was going straight to the worst of the hells, but before I could avert my eyes, I saw I didn't have to.

She was clothed under her robes, if you could call it that.

She was wearing skin-tight pants that hugged her hips in a way that would make the holiest person have sinful thoughts. I didn't want her like that—of course I didn't—Cora had been and would be the only girl for me, but gods, Scyla was beautiful.

I couldn't remember the last time I had seen a woman in pants, but even I knew it couldn't be normal for someone to look that good in them. She was wearing a flowy cream shirt that she tucked into her pants. She rolled up the sleeves over her biceps and I was five seconds away from drooling at the sight.

She turned around and seemed almost surprised for a moment to find me just sitting there watching her. I felt my cheeks flush, but I couldn't manage to say anything.

I wanted to ask her what she was doing, but I was too embarrassed she had caught me staring at her.

She watched me for a moment and then grinned, reaching under her bed. Her hand came away with a length of rope.

She watched as my eyes widened, causing her to laugh before turning away from me and taking the rope to the windows, I watched in silent fascination as she looped the end of the rope through the openings of both windows, and around the top of the two legs of the desk pushed up against the wall under the windows. After checking the rope was secure around them, she set to work securing a knot.

It took me that long to realize what she was doing. She was insane. She was going to try to climb out the window and escape. It was incredibly dangerous and stupid, but gods did I understand the urge. She hadn't been marked by the Saints yet, and if she got away, they would have no way to prove she belonged here.

If she face planted on the pavement below, which was admittedly more likely, I couldn't blame her for thinking that was a more preferable option to staying here.

She turned back to me before I could say any of that. "I suppose the second I leave, you'll probably regain that tongue of yours and raise the alarms?" she asked bluntly.

I shook my head.

"That's what they all say, but we'll see. It was nice meeting you, Rayana," she said, tossing the rope out the window. She glanced out and seemed satisfied, then grabbed the rope.

I didn't have the heart or courage to try to stop her. "I would wish you peace from whatever's been hurting you, but peace in this place could only mean a swift death." She paused to hoist herself onto the window ledge. When she looked down, I hoped it would knock some sense into her, but when she looked back at me, her smile hadn't faltered. She tugged at the rope which seemed to stay secure, then turned her attention back to me and said, "So instead, I'll wish you the fortune of meeting me again." With that she hoisted herself over the ledge.

I ran over to the window in time to see her shimmying down the last half of the rope. I couldn't believe how fast she was and how easy she had made it look. The rope hadn't so much as budged under her weight. She saluted from the ground and was off before I could so much as wave back.

I couldn't believe it.

She had done it. At least for now, she was free. She had escaped. Which left me with the rope and the beginnings of a new plan.

If I was destined to die for my crimes, dying while trying to escape was a far better fate than being executed. If I was quick, I could slip into Garrick's room, take care of him, get back here, and escape before anyone noticed anything was amiss.

If I didn't know any better, I would think Scyla had been sent by the gods themselves. This opportunity was too good to pass up. Ready or not, I would have to make my move tonight while I still had this sliver of chance of escape.

I grabbed the kitchen knife I had stolen from the kitchens earlier from its hiding spot under my pillow. I carefully put it blade-first in my robe pocket. I would have to be quick but careful. The last thing I wanted to do was accidentally slice my leg open on the way to his room. I grabbed the broom from under my bed. No one would question why I was wandering around the halls if I had a broom, and I knew how to wield it as a weapon if I needed. I hoped to take him by surprise, but if I wasn't so lucky and needed to fight him, with the knife and the broom, I had some faith in my abilities. I took a deep breath and opened the door.

I took careful quiet steps knowing things would go more smoothly if I wasn't seen. It was much easier for everyone to think I had been in my room. I didn't want witnesses if I could avoid it. If I couldn't, the broom was a convenient excuse.

The halls were quiet, which was a blessing but had me on edge. I felt like at any moment someone would discover me. They would know what I had planned and stop me before I even reached my destination.

To my shock, I made it to his door without anyone seeing me. Of course, it was night, but I had expected other people to be in the halls. There weren't even any guards.

I shook my head and took a deep breath. Now wasn't the time to question my luck, now was the time to act. I prayed to the gods to let me finish this one last sin before claiming me and turned the doorknob as slowly and quietly as I could manage. I cracked open the door and slipped inside.

Before I even closed the door, I could hear loud snores coming from the bed. My shoulders slumped in relief as I closed it behind me with a quiet click.

It was a miracle he was already sound asleep. It would make this far easier.

I turned around but stayed by the door, waiting a few moments for my eyes to adjust. Slowly his sleeping form came into focus. His blankets were rumpled around his feet and his mouth was wide open, drool slipping down his chin. He looked peaceful and I almost changed my mind, until my eyes landed on his throat and saw the locket wrapped around it, her locket.

I set the broom on the floor and crossed the room quietly. Standing over his sleeping form, I felt powerful. I grasped the handle of the knife and pulled it out of my robe. Moonlight seeping in through the window glinted on the blade, making it look far more menacing than it had in the kitchen when I stole it.

I looked down at him, hesitating. I was somewhat surprised that I had gotten this far. The fact that I hadn't been caught or called away yet meant the gods must not disapprove enough to interfere.

Yet still, I was hesitating. As much as he deserved to die, I didn't know if I was a killer. I looked down at him again and the moonlight caught her locket. It felt like a sign of approval from the gods. Why should I hesitate when I knew he hadn't hesitated when he did whatever he had to her?

As quickly as I could, I planted one leg on the bed and swung the other to his other side. He started to thrash, halfway between waking and sleeping. Before he could come to and fully start screaming, I pulled his pillow from under his head and pressed it over his face. Not hard enough to suffocate him, but hard enough to block out any screams.

The pillow muffled his screams enough, until he started screaming louder. I pushed the pillow down harder into his face as his screams became more erratic. Then I positioned the knife at his throat. I felt him still under the pillow. I had half expected him to slit his own throat on it with his thrashing. Pity for him he hadn't.

He was laying stiffly under me, so I pulled the pillow back a little saying, "If you scream, I'll slit your throat before anyone can come running."

He stayed quiet as I waited. A few moments of silence passed before I realized I hadn't asked him anything, "Say you understand."

I heard a muffled noise that was likely agreement. I pulled the pillow away slowly, prepared to make good on my threat if he got loud, but he didn't.

I watched as his eyes fell on my face, the terror on his face was quickly chased away by confusion and then anger.

"You?"

I pressed the knife into the flesh of his neck, lightly, but enough to draw blood.

"Me."

His anger gave way to panic as a trickle of blood ran down his throat. "What do you think you're doing?" He asked.

"I think I'm paying you a little visit. After all, we're both friends with Cora. I figured you'd be just as worried about her disappearance as I was-"

"She was claimed," he interrupted, glaring at me.

"So you say, but tell me," I said letting the blade glide a little further down his neck toward her locket, "if she was claimed, then how do you have her locket?"

He paled at that, and I saw his throat bob under my knife. "She gave it to me," he said quickly.

"Was that before or after she was dragged to the depths?"

"Before, obviously."

I didn't like his tone. I pressed the knife deeper into his throat. I saw his arms start to move and pressed harder, "one more move and it'll be your last. You want to walk out of here? Tell me what happened to her."

He stayed silent for a moment before relenting. "She survived the ritual. We thought the gods found her favorable, but then something went horribly wrong. The ship was attacked by sirens, and she started fighting us like she was possessed by the hells themselves. We tried to restrain her, to keep her safely on the ship, but we failed. She lost her locket in the fight, but she escaped. The last time I saw her she was being dragged to the depths by the sirens."

"Liar," I spit out. "You did something to her."

"Holy men don't lie. We thought she was holy enough to survive the seas. Clearly, we were wrong."

"I wanted the truth," I said snarling.

"That's my truth. Now let me up."

True or not, I knew it was the best I was going to get from him. I moved a little, considering my next move, whether to make it quick for him.

I shifted, moving the knife from his throat further away from his throat. He exhaled when I released the pressure and muttered, "I bet they took her cause they couldn't get to you. Her only sinful quality was being your friend."

Quicker than he could move to stop me, I pulled my knife from his throat and plunged it into his chest once, twice, three times and then I lost count. He stopped moving after the third stab, but I kept going until my arms tired of holding the knife.

When I came back to my senses, blood covered me, and my heart started to race.

His heart was still.

I didn't know how long I had been there, how long I had spent stabbing him, but his body was already slowly starting to grow cold. I needed to get out of here. I wiped my bloodied hands on his shirt. Then, wincing, I reached around his neck and undid the clasp of the necklace. Cora's locket. I grasped it carefully and fastened it around my own neck, instantly feeling a little better now that I was wearing it.

Looking down at the locket hanging on my chest, I noticed how blood soaked my clothes were. I couldn't walk out of here like that.

I looked around and spotting his wardrobe moved over to it and yanked it open. I found one of his spare white robes. It would have to do.

I pulled off my blood-soaked dress, having to stop myself from looking over my shoulder as I undressed.

I knew he was dead.

He had no pulse.

He wasn't watching, but I still felt like there were eyes on me.

I quickly wiped the rest of the blood off my hands onto my balled-up dress. Satisfied I shoved it under the bottom of his wardrobe hoping it would be a long time before anyone found it.

I finished changing as quickly as I could, careful not to stain the new robes.

I was still digesting what he had told me.

I wasn't sure I believed him. At least, I didn't want to, but the evidence was hard to deny. He had her locket, and she had last been seen at sea. It was likely the gods felt disrespected that she dared to sin and travel their seas.

If she was out there, it didn't matter if she was a monster, I had to find her. Besides, I had found out everything I was likely to from inside the Convent and while I still had a miraculous exit route, I needed to take it.

I would find somewhere to hide in one of the villages until I could gain passage on the sea. If there was a chance, however small, that I could find Cora again, I had to try.

If I could make it out alive tonight, I would spend the rest of my life chasing her. I had promised to love her even after the seas claimed her, and I had meant it.

I took a deep breath, trying to calm my racing heart. Now that I was wearing Garrick's clothes, my escape was going to be a bit more complicated. I needed to act enough like him to get back to my room unnoticed. That meant the knife and broom had to stay here and I needed to impersonate him, or at least be able to pass for him at a distance.

I tried to remember how he strutted through the halls. I pulled myself up tall, thanking the gods that he and I were of similar height and build, but this would never work if I walked the way I normally did.

I pulled the hood tight around my face and opened the door.

I made it pretty far without running into anyone, but the luck didn't hold. I rounded a corner and saw a couple of guards patrolling the halls. I felt my body wanting to freeze but forced myself to move like Garrick.

I held my breath as I approached them. To my surprise, they nodded to me and moved on. I only started breathing again when they rounded the corner.

I couldn't believe this was working.

They were the only people I ran into before making it back to my room. I yanked open the door and quickly shut it behind me. I had pulled the curtains before I left, so I was greeted with pitch darkness, but I knew the room well enough. In a few steps, I was at the window and pulled open the curtain.

My jaw dropped when I saw there was nothing there. The rope was gone. My heart raced and now I was truly panicking.

"No! No! No! Seas take me, this can't be happening! Damn it all the to hells!" I cursed softly. "It was supposed to be here!"

I heard a soft chuckle from behind me that had me stiffening in fear. "Looking for this?" the voice asked.

I whipped around and saw it was Scyla, the rope in her hands. She was back and had caught me red-handed. Probably literally, since I was hasty about brushing the blood off my hands. I was screwed and she was grinning like she knew it.

But when she stepped closer and saw my face, her grin instantly dropped.

"Blood?" she asked, pointing at my face.

Hells, I was dead. There was no denying it. I was caught. Sooner or later, everyone would know, and I was sure I wouldn't be granted a quick death. They would drag out my suffering as a teachable moment to the others girls they considered rebellious.

"Is it yours?" she asked.

I shook my head.

"Whose?"

"He deserved it."

"You weren't looking for the rope to turn me in?" she asked slowly. The realization dawned on her. "You were trying to escape."

She looked me up and down, evaluating, deciding my fate. A moment passed before she asked, "How much time do we have?"

"I don't know," I said, unsure what she was asking.

"How long has it been since you left whoever owned that blood?"

I thought hard for a moment. "Not long, but I don't know when the patrols come by or what he might be needed for."

"And what will happen when they find him? Does he live?"

"No."

"You're sure?"

I nodded.

I was shocked when a moment later she grinned, "Better for us. Dead men tell no tales."

Us. I couldn't have heard her right. Wasn't she going to go report me? "Us?" I couldn't stop myself from asking.

"You said he deserved it?"

I nodded again.

"Good enough for me."

She reached under her bed and pulled out a pack she had stowed under there. She tossed me something that I just barely managed to catch. "Put those on," she said, while she moved behind me to the window with her rope, busying herself with resecuring it.

I unfurled the bundle of fabric she had thrown to me and saw it was an outfit identical to hers. I hadn't worn pants in years, not since I was old enough to remember.

Not knowing what else to do, I did what she intended, discarding the Saints' robe I had been wearing and pulling the pants up my legs, then shrugging the shirt on. It was a bit big on me and had to be tucked into the pants. A moment later, I looked up and saw her coming toward me. I jumped back when I saw a dagger in her hand.

I relaxed a little when she flipped it over, sheathed it, and handed it to me. I knew from the buckles that it was supposed to attach to something, but I had no idea how to secure it.

She watched me stare at it for a moment before bending down on one knee in front of me and grabbing my thigh. I yelped in surprise, almost losing my balance. I just barely managed to stop myself from toppling over onto my bed as she set to work fastening the sheath to my thigh.

"We're going too slow," she muttered to herself as she finished fastening it. "Do you know how to use it?" she asked.

"A little."

"Good enough." She finished tightening it, standing up quickly. "Alright, out we go."

"Where?" I asked.

She looked at me confused, "Out the window, of course."

"Yes, but after that?"

"Assuming we make it, we take to the seas."

I gasped. She pulled me to the window, pulling me up on the ledge with her. "The seas? We can't! There're sirens out there and the holy men on patrol. It's their domain. You can't be serious."

I had meant to go to the seas eventually, but not right now when the alarm would soon be raised and everyone would be on the lookout for anyone suspicious. I had meant to lie low first.

"*You* can't be serious." She pulled my body to hers and starting tying the rope around us. She pulled me flush to her body and I gasped. "You can murder a man in cold blood but going to the sea is where you draw the line?" She pulled the rope taut, eliminating the last whisper of space between her bodies. It took all my strength not to look down at her chest that was pressed against mine.

"This isn't how you did it," I pointed out.

"Well, unless you have experience with ropes, we'll be caught and hung before sunrise if you try to climb down, so we're improvising."

I looked down quickly and regretted it. It was a long way down. "Are you sure it's safe?"

"No," she said, testing the rope at the window. It didn't budge.

"Is this really a good idea?" I asked again, trying to force myself to breathe.

"Odds are we'll make it, but either way, you're free."

I nodded. She was right. Either way, I might die tonight. If I stayed, I was dead for sure. I didn't know how long it would take them to figure out it was me, but my missing clothes would eventually point back to me. It might take a couple of days, but they would find out eventually. They would do their room sweeps and find I was the only one missing her extra set of clothes.

That I had gotten this far in the first place was a small miracle.

Tonight, I had a choice. I could risk my life for a chance at freedom or preserve it for a couple more days for a humiliating, painful death. It wasn't a choice, not really.

Scyla saw the resolve in my eyes and asked, "Ready?"

"As I'll ever be."

"Hold tight."

I couldn't do anything else with how tightly she tied us, so I obeyed, lacing my arms around her. She did the same, gripping me tight.

For a fraction of a moment, I let myself think of Cora. I hadn't been this close to another woman since I last saw her. I hadn't even hugged anyone. It felt wrong, even more so because the night had a feeling of rightness to it. It felt like this was my destiny.

I reminded myself I was doing this for Cora and that, gods willing, if I ever found her, she was sure to forgive me.

I was doing this for her.

"On three," Scyla said, and I nodded. She gripped me tighter. "One."

She moved closer to the edge, and I tried to steady myself for what was coming.

She moved suddenly, pulling me with her over the ledge.

I barely heard her say, "Two," over the rush of the wind as we flew through the air.

We were flying.

I let out a delighted whoop until I saw the ground quickly approaching.

Falling.

We were falling.

We were going to die, but at least I would die free.

I closed my eyes, not wanting to watch my end coming to meet me. A moment later, all the air was knocked out of me as a force squeezed tight around my stomach. I couldn't breathe against the tug. My eyes whipped open, and I saw that we were hanging together within a foot of the ground.

We were alive.

She maneuvered her arm to her thigh, grabbed her dagger, at sawed at the ropes. It took a minute, but she cut us loose. I was ready to kiss the ground, thankful to be alive, but she grabbed my hand and pulled, starting to run.

"But the rope," I said quickly, trying to pull her back. "You can't leave it there, they'll know."

She turned her head a moment, still pulling me forward, and laughed, "And they'll find the body too and notice we're missing. They're already going to know. Better to leave the rope so they know we didn't have help."

She was right. I hadn't thought about it, but they would punish everyone who had ever smiled in my direction if they thought someone else had anything to do with our escape. Leaving the proof that we made it out on our own might save the others. Maybe instead of punishing them, they would just cover it up and say the seas claimed us.

We ran faster, wanting to put as much distance between ourselves and the Convent as quickly as possible.

We had to be out of here by the time they came looking. If we weren't anywhere to be found, they couldn't make an example of us.

Without us being around, they would tell everyone that I had been driven mad by Cora's loss and killed a holy man before the sea claimed me for my sins. It was the perfect cover because, after all, escape from the Convent was impossible.

They would cover it up as long as we were gone by sunrise, gone before the warning bells were rung.

That was our only hope. We ran and ran faster than I ever had in my life.

# Chapter Twelve
## Ray

As we grew closer to the pier, I was starting to have hope. I could almost taste freedom when two things happened.

The first was Scyla taking a sharp right turn away from the pier.

The second was seeing that there were guards on the pier with torches, seemingly looking for something. I hadn't heard the alarm bells, but that meant nothing.

There was a good chance they were looking for us, but even if they weren't, if they found us fleeing the Convent, they would just drag us back. It would only take one glimpse of my marked skin to know I was the Convent's property. These men wouldn't think twice about bringing me back.

The mark of the Saints of Santerra, a large anchor, was etched with ink onto my left shoulder. Right now, it was hidden, but these were Isle guards; they would know what to look for.

Scyla didn't have the same problem, but if she were seen with me, caught helping me, she'd be in just as much trouble. Even if they believed she had never been the property of the Saints, she would be branded a criminal, a thief for stealing the property of the Saints, and would have forfeited her right to her life. Whether she would be made to serve in the sanctuary or punished in another manner would be up to the holy men to decide.

We couldn't be caught, I couldn't drag her down with me.

"Where in the nine hells are we going?" I asked.

"Shhhh," she whispered harshly, urging me to hurry as we wound down the cliff path leading away from the pier.

"I thought you had a ship," I rushed out as quietly as possible. Not tripping on the path and keeping a quick pace were taking most of my energy. I didn't dare take my eyes off the path to look at her.

"I do," she said, "but we need to hurry."

"But the pier's back there."

"And crawling with guards."

"So, where are we going?"

"We never use the pier. Just a little further."

As we rounded a bend in the path, I saw we had arrived at a little cove. My jaw dropped when I saw the only boat on the water was a miniscule rowboat that was barely big enough for two people.

That's it. I was going to die.

If they didn't catch us before we got out to sea, the sharks or the sirens would get us for sure.

"You have to be kidding me. We're going to die. I should have taken my chances in the Convent. This is suicide."

She looked at me, concern coloring her features. "Can't you swim?"

I gawked at her; she was mad. She was truly mad. "Swim? Of course I can swim. I live on a damned island, but I can't swim faster than a shark."

She jumped into the boat still laughing. The boat rocked dangerously under her sudden weight. There was no way that thing was seaworthy.

"The sharks won't bother us."

"The sirens then. I can't out-swim a siren."

She laughed at that, "You won't have to. You'll find that the sirens quite like me." She held out her hand but I frantically shook my head.

She was a lunatic. There was no way this woman was sane, and no way I was getting in the boat with her.

"I can't believe I trusted you. Where would we even go in this thing? You said we were hitting the seas. I thought you had a ship!" I was panicking now.

She looked at me confused, "I do."

"No one in their right mind would call this a ship."

She blinked at me a moment before she started howling in laughter. She was the picture of a madwoman.

"What's so funny?" I asked, glaring at her.

"This isn't my ship. This is a rowboat. The ship's out there. Now, hurry up and get in."

Feeling embarrassed and only a small amount more at ease, I stepped in, and it started to rock. She quickly grabbed my hips, steadying me. I nodded my thanks as I slowly lowered myself.

"Come on," she said, handing me a paddle. "You know how to row?"

I nodded. In theory I did. It couldn't be that hard.

"Then get to it. We're running out of time."

I looked up and saw with concern that she was right. The sky was already lightening. I didn't know how much longer we had until the sun rose, but I knew that with dawn would come the warning bells. With dawn, they would notice Garrick missing. With dawn, every port and pier on the isle would be locked down on high alert. Any unregistered ship leaving would be considered suspect and an enemy. If we didn't leave before then, I was dooming not only myself, but Scyla and whoever else was on her ship.

I followed her lead and started rowing. It was so much harder than I imagined it would be. Before we got halfway out of the cove, she took over for me. I was embarrassed to find we moved faster without my help.

With her manning both oars, in no time we were exiting the cove. As the sky opened up before us, I saw what she was referring to and my jaw dropped. Her ship was massive. It was a fortress on the water. There were more cannons than I could count and numerous rowboats like ours hung from the sides.

"How are we getting up there?" I asked as she approached the ship and it rose up tall over us.

She laughed and nodded toward the ship. I followed her gaze and saw the rope. I groaned, but when I looked closer, I saw that at least this rope had rungs like a ladder to make climbing more possible. Without the rungs, I would have probably drowned before I could climb the rope well enough to pull myself onto the ship's deck.

She had me go first, and when I occasionally wobbled, she steadied me.

When I got to the top, there was a gap between the ladder and the side of the ship, but I heard Scyla bang on the side, and a hand came down. I grabbed it and they pulled me up.

"Thank the goddess you're back," they called over the side. "We saw the guards and were getting worried–" She stopped short when she finished pulling me up and saw I wasn't who she was expecting. She looked startled and dropped my hand. I stumbled forward, further onto the ship. Before I righted myself, I heard another bang, and she moved around me to help Scyla. I looked at her then and was shocked to see she somehow managed to be even more muscled than my companion. She was tall with long unruly brown hair with the tallest hat I had ever seen. It was black and oddly shaped with the etching of a sea monster on the side.

"If you keep bringing new recruits, we're going to have to get an even bigger ship," she grumbled, hoisting my roommate onto the deck. She landed more gracefully than I had.

I saw Scyla was grinning.

"We have plenty of room and you know it."

The woman looked at me, taking in the state I was in, and her features softened. "Convent girl?" she asked.

I froze, not knowing what to say.

Scyla put her hand on my shoulder and said, "It's okay, you're safe here."

Comforted, I nodded. "The Convent was the only home I remember."

"How long were you there?" the woman asked.

"Almost all my life, twenty of my twenty-five years if you're trying to age me."

Scyla laughed, and I was surprised to see that the woman did too.

"What made you want to leave now?" she asked, not unkindly, but it was a stupid question.

"I've been wanting to leave my whole life."

"But why now?" she asked again.

"I didn't have much of a choice," I said simply, hoping to avoid the rest of the questions that I knew were coming. I needed her to like me, to trust me. I needed her to let me stay. If she wanted to send me away, I would have nowhere else to go. Telling her I murdered a man would hardly make a good first impression.

She crossed her arms and turned to Scyla. "What did I tell you about kidnapping people?"

She grinned. "It wasn't me this time, honest. She basically kidnapped herself. I rescued her."

She turned back to me and asked, "Did you need rescuing?"

I nodded.

"Why?"

When I didn't answer, Scyla spoke up. "She gutted one of those heretics like a fish, with no exit plan. She's got guts and the heart of a pirate. She's one of us."

Pirates. They were pirates. I couldn't believe I hadn't realized it sooner. There wasn't much mention of pirates, except for one all-female crew. The Saints talked about the infamous Daughters of the Deep with the same disgust they usually saved for sirens.

The Daughters of the Deep sailed the sea fighting the Saints. I wasn't sure if all pirates were like them, but hearing these pirates refer to the Saints, the holy men, the god chosen, as heretics brought me as much pleasure as it did hope.

The pirate turned to me and simply asked, "Why?"

"He abused women."

"And you know this for certain?"

I nodded. "He admitted it, and he had my—" I paused for a moment, "my best friend's necklace. They claimed she was lost to the sea on their holy mission, but he had her necklace."

The pirate and Scyla exchanged a look. "Well, it's going to be a long night," she said before looking at the sky and scowling. "Correction, a long morning. You should have been quicker. I'm guessing we might have company soon."

She turned and started calling out orders. I looked around, amazed as the previously empty ship swarmed with activity. There were people coming out of several doors I hadn't noticed before, and most amazingly of all, they were all women.

I gawked at them for a moment, before chastising myself and looking around for a way I could be useful. I had brought the hells to their doorstep, so the least I could do was help them escape. Scyla still stood at my side, so I asked her, "What can I do?"

"Nothing. You ran like the hells were chasing you and made it here safely. You ended one of their worthless lives. You've done enough for tonight. I would bid you rest, but since you're new here and told us quite the tale, unfortunately, we have to keep you up a bit longer. As soon as we make it the open sea and are in the clear, Tess will want to talk to you more."

"Tess? As in Tess the Terrible of the Daughters of the Deep?" I squeaked out.

She laughed at that, "Tess as in the woman you just met. Tess the Terrible Pain in the Ass is more like it. Known more formally as our captain. She just goes by Tess, though." She shook her head and repeated quietly, "Tess the Terrible." She let out a sigh. "Gods she's going to have a terrible ego."

# Chapter Thirteen

## Ray

When Captain Tess determined we had gone far enough to be safe, she had someone take the helm from her and guided me into her office.

Scyla came with us, and as I got settled in a chair, another woman walked in. As she strode over to Captain Tess's desk, I noticed something strange about her movements, but I couldn't decide what.

She looked normal enough. She was on the shorter side with pale skin and dark hair. She was dressed like the other pirates, but unlike the others, her movements radiated power. It gave me a chill I couldn't explain. If I hadn't already met Captain Tess, I would've assumed this woman was the captain herself.

She reached the desk and instead of sitting in one of the free chairs, hopped up and sat on it, her feet dangling. She looked over the desk at Captain Tess and said, "I thought we were going for informal?"

The captain grinned, shaking her head, "Fine, fine." She pulled a bottle out from her desk and turned to me. "I try to act tough for the new recruits."

"And I'm sure it used to work," the other woman said, laughing. Her laugh was beautiful, almost too rich to listen to. "Before me, when you didn't have anyone to call you on your dramatics."

"Lucky for your ego, you have us," Scyla chimed in.

The captain took a dramatic swig from her bottle before offering it to the woman. She declined and the captain stoppered the bottle and tossed it to Scyla who caught the bottle by the neck with one hand.

"Show off," the captain said, grinning.

Scyla smiled and took a swig before offering me the bottle. I went to shake my head, but Scyla added, "You'll want some to fortify you. It's been a long morning and will be longer still before you can sleep."

"Plus, it'll make the conversation easier," the captain chimed in.

"If the girl doesn't want to drink, she doesn't have to," said the other woman.

I trusted Scyla though, so I took a swig from the bottle. Unfortunately, it was a lot harsher than the drink they occasionally offered us at the Convent. It burned my throat going down and I started coughing. I handed the bottle back to Scyla who started clapping me on the back.

The Captain grabbed a glass of something else and walked over to me while the strange woman scolded her. "See? Not everyone is built to drink like a fish like you two."

The captain held out the glass, but I hesitated.

"It's just water," she said.

I took the glass from her with a nod that I hoped showed my gratitude and started to drink. The other woman chose that moment to turn around, giving me my first full look at her. I saw her eyes for the first time and choked up the water I had been drinking.

It took me a minute of them fussing over me to regain my ability to breathe.

When I did, I quickly said, "I'm so sorry, but your eyes..." I trailed off, not knowing what to say or ask. They were a vibrant blue and swirling, and there was no way it was natural.

"Ah," she said, looking away from me. "They're a gift from Nema."

Shame crept up in me. I didn't understand what she meant, but I should have known better than to rudely point them out. "I'm so sorry. I shouldn't have asked."

I turned to Scyla, who said, "It's okay. Mel knows you didn't mean anything by it, right?"

She nodded quickly and looked up at me with a sad smile. "Everyone else around here is used to them. I forget they aren't normal sometimes."

"What happened?" I asked before I could think better of it.

"A lot of bad things, and then a really good thing," she said, lacing her hand with the captain's at her side.

"We have a lot to tell you," Captain Tess said.

"Understatement of the century," Scyla quipped.

"We'll try to be brief. I'm sure you're exhausted," the captain told me.

I was, but I needed to hear what she had to say.

"I'll be okay," I assured her.

The woman with the eyes snorted, turning to the captain. "She'll fit right in. She's already too stubborn for her own good."

"Just like a pirate," Scyla said, elbowing me, making me laugh.

The woman turned back to me with a look of alarm. "I didn't introduce myself, did I?"

"That's Mel," Scyla said quickly.

"Short for Melody," Mel said with a smile.

"And even shorter for the melody that plays in my heart," the captain said, grinning at Mel.

I blinked. I couldn't have heard that right. They were holding hands, but surely that was just a show of support. Then the captain leaned in and kissed her on the lips for longer than was comfortable to watch. I couldn't look away. I only tore my eyes away when I heard Scyla making exaggerated gagging noises next to me.

"Get a room!" she yelled at them.

They pulled away, Mel's cheeks flushed, the pair wearing matching grins.

"These are all my rooms," Captain Tess retorted.

"Yeah, yeah, look at me, I'm Tess and I own a ship and all of its rooms cause I'm a big fancy pirate captain with a stupidly tall hat," Scyla said mockingly.

We all laughed, and then laughed harder when Tess added, "You forgot to add incredibly good-looking."

"As tall as your ego," Mel said playfully, before adding, "just the way I like them."

We all laughed at that, but when I caught my breath, before we moved on, I had to ask about them. It seemed like they were together, like they were openly in love and happy. For that to be a reality for two women was unimaginable.

"Are you two...?" I asked, pointing between them, not sure what term to use.

The captain's eyes narrowed, but Mel asked more patiently, "In love? Yes, we are."

"Is that going to be a problem?" the captain asked harshly, and I felt like I was finally getting my first glimpse at the famed Captain Tess the Terrible.

I saw Mel squeeze the captain's hand, and the simple loving gesture brought tears to my eyes.

Scyla cleared her throat, and I turned to her. "I could have better prepared you, but we didn't have time. Needless to say, things are different here. On this ship, we don't subscribe to the same ideals of the Isles. It can be a little jarring at first."

It wasn't the captain and her lover that were too much for me, it was everything. I couldn't believe I was safe here. I hadn't believed that there was anywhere where it was safe to be a woman, and now the thought that it was safe here to be yourself and love whoever you wanted had snapped the last of my composure.

"No, no. That's not it," I rushed to say through my tears. "I—you don't understand, I didn't think a woman loving a woman could be safe anywhere." I paused, drawing up my strength before continuing, "The man I killed didn't take my best friend, he took the woman I loved."

Scyla's eyes widened, Tess cursed, and Mel's lips fell into a frown. She took a step forward and asked, "What do you mean they took her?"

"She went out on a holy mission with those men and never returned. They say she was called by the sea, but I know that can't be the whole story."

They all exchanged a glance before Mel crossed the distance and pulled me into a hug.

I was surprised and stayed rigid for a moment before hugging her back. She was right, I needed it.

"It seems we have a lot to tell you," Tess said.

Mel let go of me and turned back to Tess, saying, "We really should take it easy on the girl. I'm sure she's exhausted. Can the welcome speech wait?"

Captain Tess shrugged and said, "Fair enough. We've all had a long night and a longer morning. The short version is what I'm sure you already know. No matter what the Saints say of the sirens or us, the Saints are the only true monsters on these waters."

"Ray wouldn't be here if she didn't know that," Scyla said.

She was right. I wouldn't have left if I thought the Saints were anything less than monsters.

"What you don't know, and what we've been trying to prove to no avail for the last year, is that the Saints are responsible for the increase in sirens."

"What?" That couldn't possibly be true.

"It's not quite that simple," Mel said.

"They're the catalyst," the captain argued. "They came and stole the Isles right from under our noses and then suddenly we had a siren problem."

"There were always sirens," Mel added.

"But they weren't bothering the Isles until the Saints came."

The captain turned back to me. "The sirens didn't attack unprovoked before the Saints came around, and I very much still believe that to be true. The increase in siren attacks is the Saints' fault. They spare merchants, fisherman, and us. They usually only attack the Saints, but somehow they've buried that fact and used the attacks to sow fear and sink their claws into the Isles."

"We were meant to believe it was just a coincidence that the sirens increased after the Saints came," Scyla said. "Unfortunately, people believe what they want, and believing the Saints had the answers was easier."

"Easier if you're okay with nothing changing," the captain said, frustrated.

"And a lot them are," Scyla said. "They put their heads in the sand and think if things don't change for the better, at least they won't get worse. It's ignorant, but it would take a lot to wake up Santerra."

"Lucky for the people, I'm a whole lot," the captain said, grinning before she turned back to me and grew more serious. "We have reason to believe that the Saints' abuse of women is causing the increase in sirens and the increase in siren attacks."

I thought about it for a moment before saying slowly, "That makes sense. Angry women are much more likely to sin and be called to the sea."

"That's–" Tess started and then tried again, "not quite what I meant. Sirens aren't sinful women. They aren't cursed by the gods, they're blessed by them."

Mel took over then. "When a woman is turned into a siren, it's a blessing from the sea herself, and only happens when the only alternative is death."

I wasn't sure if I believed their theory, but I did believe them that the Saints were monsters. The part I was struggling with was believing that they were creating the problem they were trying to fight. The Saints were cruel, certainly, but actively plaguing the Isles with sirens... I wanted to believe it was too evil even for them.

"And you think the Saints..." I trailed off, not wanting to finish the horrible thought that they could be abusing and possibly killing the women they took on their holy missions. I knew most of the women didn't return from their missions, but we had always been told they were moved to other Isles. I felt stupid now for never questioning that.

The captain nodded, "We think they bring women onto their ships and abuse them."

"Which attracts the attention of the seas, and the sirens are sent to deal with the Saints," Mel said.

"They save some of the women," Scyla added quickly.

"But not all?" I asked, my heart sinking as I thought about how happy Cora looked the last time I saw her.

Mel shook her head. "They do their best, but sometimes they aren't quick enough, and other times they're only just in time to offer a choice, and a new siren is born."

If what they were saying was true, then my only hope of ever seeing Cora again was that Garrick had been telling the truth, and she had been turned into a siren. It was a fate that I still struggled to see as anything less than worse than death despite what they were telling me.

"So, you think she could be out there somewhere?" I asked, rubbing her locket for strength.

I looked at Scyla who nodded quickly. "If she's half as strong as you, I'm sure she is."

"Cora was stronger than me in every way that mattered."

"Then I'm sure she's out there somewhere," Scyla reassured me.

They could all see it was hardly reassuring though, so Mel said, "I'm not sure what you're picturing, but it's not as bad as that."

"She might be out there, alone and afraid," I said quietly. "And no matter how far I go, I won't find her down there."

The captain quickly interjected, "No, no. It's not like that. They travel in packs."

"Pods," Mel corrected.

"Yes, love, sorry. Pods." When I looked confused, she added, "You could say Mel here is our resident siren expert, but yes, they travel in pods. You never see a solo siren. They take care of their own fiercely."

It was some consolation at least that if she was still out there, she wouldn't be alone or afraid.

They could tell that was about all I could handle, though, and I was grateful to them for ending the meeting after a few more minutes spent trying to reassure me.

Scyla led me straight from the captain's office to my sleeping quarters, a cozy-looking hammock across from hers.

I slid into it without a second thought and as soon as I rolled over the exhaustion of the day and the rocking of the waves lulled me to sleep.

# CHAPTER FOURTEEN
# Ray

I worried the other girls would take a while to warm up to me, but I was shocked to find that most of them understood me immediately. Most of them had come from the Convent too and, like me, had somehow managed to escape. They called themselves Convent brats because the Saints couldn't beat the bad behavior out of them.

I felt right at home and was proud to call myself a Convent brat. I had been raised by the Convent, and like these other women, was proud of the fact that I had made it out, and that I hadn't lost myself or my fire along the way.

I was even prouder to be called a Daughter.

I had thought the Daughters of the Deep was just a name they sailed under, but Captain Tess took it seriously, reminding us all that we were family, united as sisters against the Saints of Santerra. They had a lot of names for the Saints, but most just called them the heretics or the White Robes. It was going to take some time to get used to how freely everyone spoke here.

The girls here spoke the secret anxieties of my own heart. I had felt for years that the Saints were cruel without reason and that they abused those under their power. The Saints proclaimed it made them strong, but I always felt that wielding their power to hurt those below them made them weak.

It only took a few days of sailing with the Daughters to be content in the fact that the gods intended for me to be here.

Nowhere in my twenty-five years of life had I felt more at home than I did on this ship.

Scyla took me under her wing and introduced me to everyone and helped me learn the ropes, both figuratively and literally. Ropes, much to my chagrin, were turning out to be a large part of life on the sea.

# Chapter Fifteen
# Ray

At the end of my first week, Scyla came to find me after my duties were done for the day. I had just laid down when she popped in asking, "Where, oh, where is my ray of sunshine?"

I groaned at her, fighting a grin at the nickname. It had been rare that we were addressed by name in the Convent. Having a nickname was almost unthinkable. Before Scyla, Cora had been the only one who called me Ray. It was bittersweet to know that Cora would most definitely like Scyla.

Scyla looked down at me with a grin. "Moan all you want, you know you love me. After all, I'm your closest friend and favorite savior."

I rolled my eyes. "If by 'favorite' you mean *only*, then yes."

"Don't sell yourself short. You have other friends."

I laughed at that. "You know that's not what I meant."

"I know you're not belittling my damsel-rescuing skills, so I must be your favorite."

"Have you rescued any damsels lately?" I asked, making a show of looking around. I was hardly a damsel, and she knew it. She *had* rescued me, though. Without her, I would have likely died in the Convent, whether in body or soul; they would have killed me even if they didn't end my life.

"True, true," she conceded. "You're too lanky to be a proper damsel."

"Hey! That's muscle."

She eyed me skeptically. "Sure it is."

"Well, with more days like this, I'm sure it will be in no time. It's no joke here."

"Aye aye, I'll drink to that. Come on, Tess is waiting."

I jumped up immediately and hurriedly straightened my shirt and brushed some of the ever-present dirt off my pants. "Why didn't you say so?" I asked feeling frantic.

I had only been on the ship for a few days, and I owed the captain my life as much as I owed it to Scyla. I hadn't seen much of Captain Tess since that first night since my duties were mostly belowdecks, but she was the reason I was still here. Captain Tess was the one who agreed to let me sail with her crew.

I froze, panic leeching the color from my face. What if she changed her mind? It was clear I wasn't a natural sailor or a natural pirate, but I was doing my best. I was a hard worker and an even faster learner and I was determined to stay here. It was the only place that had ever felt like home, and I wasn't prepared to lose it.

Scyla must have seen some of the thoughts flitting over my face since she quickly added, "Relax, she just wants to officially welcome you to the family."

"Didn't she already do that?"

"Your first night?" Scyla asked.

"Yeah, she told me all about the ship and the crew."

"That whole song and dance is just the intro, not the welcome. She learned a while back to hold off on the actual welcome party for a week. One week on this ship is enough to tell the pirates from the damsels."

"And what am I?"

"As convincing of a damsel as you made, in your chest beats the heart of a pirate through and through. I would trust you with my life but not my coin."

I laughed at that. I had learned quickly that that sort of statement was a compliment coming from her.

She grinned back and said, "Let's get a move on. It was a long day, and I'm more than ready to drink my fill."

# Chapter Sixteen

## Ray

The captain herself handed me my first mug of ale, saying, "Congratulations, Pirate Rayana. Welcome to the Daughters."

I was touched beyond words and just stared at the mug she offered.

Scyla clapped me on the back and said, "It's not poison, just take it."

I did with a grin. "Thank you, Captain."

She smiled, "You can call me just about anything you like, but my name's Tess. You're welcome to use it."

I wasn't about to ask what names were off limits, but the gleam in Scyla's eye told me that she was up to no good when she said, "Con–"

The Captain, Tess, turned and glared daggers at her. Scyla just raised her eyebrows and continued, "–trary to what you might say, I know you love being called Captain."

Addie, an outgoing, caring redhead I had seen around a few times, came over, handing mugs to Scyla and Tess. I hadn't even noticed that Tess didn't have her own drink, yet. It had to be a breach in etiquette or at least protocol to be served before the Captain.

"I'm so sorry–" I started gesturing to her drink, "I should've waited for you to be served."

Tess smiled and waved a hand. "We're all family here. That's the Convent talking, and I'm determined to drill the manners right out of you."

I laughed at that.

Melody moved from the other side of the room over to us and took up a place at Tess's side. She planted a quick kiss on Tess's lips before grabbing the mug Tess was holding and taking a deep drink from it.

"Besides," Tess said with a grin. "You'd be waiting a while since this one takes everything I own."

"Nothing you wouldn't willingly give, Contessa."

Tess narrowed her eyes at Scyla who was reaching out to high five Melody.

"Contessa's her full name, and I'm sure she'd much rather be called anything else under the sun," Addie said to me in a mock whisper.

Tess raised her voice, the rest of the room quieting instantly. "If any of you sea scoundrels even think of calling me that, I'll have your swords."

I paled, but everyone else went back to their conversations, ignoring us again. I looked at Scyla who said, "She's joking, bad as she is at it."

Scyla elbowed Tess who said, "Hey! I'm your feared captain."

"Yes, you're oh-so scary," Melody said with a smile and booped her on the nose. "A fearful, deadly pirate."

"I stole your heart, didn't I? I must be a damn good pirate."

Scyla took my arm as Tess leaned in to kiss Melody.

"Let's give them a minute. Why don't I introduce you to Addie?"

We both knew I had already met Addie, but Scyla took me over there anyway. Addie then introduced me to a quiet girl that I hadn't met yet. I had seen watching me during my time on the ship, though. Addie introduced her as Neta, our eyes in the sky, since she was usually posted in the crow's nest. She was on the smaller side and managed to climb ropes quicker than anyone else on board.

I had been curious about her the few times I had been on deck and saw her looking down at me. She didn't look like a lot of the other Isle girls. I guessed from her mannerisms she was probably a Convent brat like me, but she had light brown skin I hadn't often seen, fairer than Scyla's, but darker than mine, even with the sun I was getting. She had dark brown hair that she always kept braided and I had never seen her smile.

I wondered if being off duty would change that, but it didn't. She was comfortable here, that much was clear, but she didn't let loose. Her hair was still tightly braided, and she still didn't smile.

Of course, a lot of the other Convent brats didn't let loose either. The Convent beat the joy out of you, so we weren't a loud bunch, but you could tell the others were enjoying themselves and they smiled. Neta apparently still didn't, even at a party.

I drank a little with the others, and then a bit more, until the ale had us halfway to seasickness. By then, most of the crew had crawled off to their hammocks to sleep the effects off.

I was lagging but didn't want to seem ungrateful. After all, they were celebrating me.

I was glad I stayed when Tess called for a toast to me. "To our newest sister. Welcome home, Ray."

Everyone echoed the toast as they drank with me. I felt the warmth spread in my chest at their acceptance and knew it wasn't just from the ale.

Whether or not I had been searching for it, I had found my home. I just wished Cora was here with me to enjoy it.

I had made myself a promise that I intended to keep, however. By sin or by sail, I would find her.

# Chapter Seventeen
## Ray

In my second week of sailing, Tess had me on deck more often, learning the ropes.

A few days in, I saw my first siren.

The tail in the water had me panicking, despite everything I knew. I tried to relax, to stop the panic, but the fear had been drilled into me, and apparently old habits died screaming because I started to yell, "Sirens!"

A couple of the others on deck ran over to watch, excited to see them, and it helped me to breathe a little. The rest kept working. No one else was scared. I was going to be okay. They weren't the enemy. They weren't going to hurt us. I took a deep breath and walked back to the railing.

No one else was panicking, and they had all sailed way longer than I had. If the sirens were that dangerous, the pirates wouldn't still be here.

As I watched, there were another two tails that joined the first to wave at our ship. The girls next to me giggled and waved back.

The tails disappeared, and then I watched, frozen there, as their faces emerged. They seemed to be watching us, evaluating. I held my breath, trying to remind myself that the rest of the crew was still working. No one else was worried and it was going to be okay. The sirens weren't our enemies.

The others trusted the truce we had with the sirens.

The more I looked at them without anything bad happening, the easier it was to trust this fact, too. They were beautiful of course, but I didn't feel any inclination to dive into the water with them, so I knew I was still thinking for myself.

I was still a little skeptical, though. The sirens' power awed me, but I couldn't look away. When they started swimming again and more joined them, I continued to stare.

Watching them gliding below the surface, I tried to take in their faces. Now that I was calmer, I was doing what I should have been in the first place and observing them, hoping to see a familiar face. From what I could tell through the water, Cora wasn't with them. I couldn't decide if I was relieved or disappointed.

One of the sirens surfaced again, and I could have sworn she winked at me before turning and diving back into the water, waving her tail to me as she went. I gasped and heard Scyla laugh behind me.

Without tearing my eyes from the water, I asked, "What just happened? Tell me I'm seeing things."

She laughed. "Some are more playful than others. Looks like you caught her eye."

"But she didn't try anything." I turned around after the sea calmed again. "Why do they leave us alone?"

Scyla shrugged. "It depends on who you ask. The captain says they're angels, the holy men say they're devils. Who knows what their motives are?"

"What about you? What do you think?"

"I think they're more like us than I would care to admit. Who hasn't had the urge to drown a few men?"

I laughed at that. I couldn't not. There were quite a few 'holy men' that the world would be a better place without.

"I don't think they're all good or all bad. Best to be cautious around them. Unspoken truce or not, you wouldn't catch me in the water with any of them on purpose, but I know the White Robes' lies aren't true. I know that if they want the sirens dead, that's a good enough reason for me to want to protect them."

"The enemy of my enemy," I said, grinning.

"Absolutely! Plus, the sirens are definitely much better to look at that any one of those holy men."

I didn't respond, unable to find the words, and just watched her walk away. Hearing others talk openly about appreciating other women was still wild to me. I don't know if I would ever get used to it, if I would ever stop worrying about the consequences, but seeing how freely these women talked and laughed with one another gave me hope.

Seeing the captain with Melody, seeing their love, was enough to make even the hardest heart soften and start to hope.

# Chapter Eighteen
## Ray

"Man the decks!" came a loud cry from above. I rolled over, trying to jump out of the hammock, but got tangled in my haste. "Daughters to your stations!" came another cry, Scyla this time.

I twisted myself and the hammock back around and jumped out, grabbing my dagger just in case and quickly making my way to the deck along with the others.

We had drilled that command so many times that part of me wondered if this was just that—a drill—but I felt the cannon before I made it above deck.

This was real.

I bounded out onto the deck and saw the enemy ship full of Saints and froze. A moment later, Neta grabbed me, and I remembered myself. "With me," she said, and I followed behind her. She made her way to the mast, pausing for a brief moment to check on me.

"Go, I'm ready."

With that, she ascended the rope to the crow's nest. My job was simple. I was here to make sure that if gods forbid anyone made it onto our decks, they didn't get close to Neta.

I watched as she pulled a bow from her back and quickly nocked an arrow. The arrows were dipped in something that Flora, the ship's alchemist and sometimes healer, had given her that ignited when fired. Neta was our eye in the sky and our fire from above. She was integral in protecting our ship, which made having the hopefully unnecessary job of protecting her a little less upsetting.

I didn't mind protecting her, but I wanted to prove my worth, and in all the time Scyla had been sailing with the Daughters, no one had ever breached the ship. I highly doubted today would change that.

I itched to help my sisters shore up the ship or fire the cannons at the Saints, but I knew better than to disobey Tess in my first actual fight.

Neta's arrows were hitting home. The Saints' mainsail was up in flames and I watched as fire engulfed one of the Saints. He dove overboard in his panic to douse the flames.

He surfaced, and I could see the relief on his face from here. Then I noticed the water moving around him. One minute he was there, and the next, he was gone with a cut-off scream.

I watched the water closely, waiting, until I spotted what I was looking for.

A tail.

Sirens.

I almost moved to get a closer look, but I stopped myself.

Then I heard their song, and fear spiked in me for just a moment before it was replaced with calm. Their song was beautiful, but not enough to make me move.

The calm I felt didn't come from their song itself, but the splashes coming from the other ship as, one by one, the Saints dove into the water and were picked off by sirens.

Then, a boat dropped from their ship, and I tensed, wondering if some of them were somehow immune to the sirens' song. For a moment, I worried they might get away, until a cheer rang out and I noticed what I hadn't before. Scyla along with a few other of our crewmates were on the Saints' rowboat coming our way with food and barrels full of either water or ale. If I was a betting pirate, I would say the majority were ale.

# CHAPTER NINETEEN
# Ray

We drank even more that night than we had at my welcome party. I had enough to drink that when most had cleared out, leaving just me, Tess, Mel, Scyla, Addie, and Neta. Surrounded by the people that were quickly becoming my family, I finally asked a question I hadn't had the courage to voice until now. "What brings you all here?"

I knew, of course, that they were all refugees in some way, shape, or form like I was, but I didn't know their stories– not really–and I was dying to know.

"The sirens, in one way or another," Tess said with a smile at Mel, who smiled back softly.

"Are we really doing this?" Scyla asked.

"Doing what?" I asked her.

"Giving our whole backstories. I haven't had enough to drink for this."

"If you had any more, you'd have drunk more than the ocean," Addie called out.

Scyla chuckled and looked around at the group. Tess and Mel were murmuring to each other. Neta was sitting off to the side watching the sea through the porthole, not paying us any mind. I looked at Addie and noticed she grew distinctly uncomfortable the moment Scyla met her eye.

Scyla shrugged, "Fine, fine, don't all rush to talk at once. I'll go first, but only if we all share." No one said anything, so she asked again, "Agreed?"

"Sure," Tess said.

"Fine with me," Mel added.

"Alright," Addie said.

We all turned to Neta, who said, "I'm probably the least interesting story here, but fine."

I was surprised to hear her say so much all at once. I highly doubted I would be bored by whatever she had to say.

"It's about time anyway," Tess said. "Ray's proved herself. She's a true Daughter and a true pirate through and through. It's time she heard more of our stories."

"I thought you'd told me pretty much everything by now?" I asked.

She shrugged, "I told you what you needed to know, but we don't tell most people everything until they've proven themselves. For the same reason you didn't get a welcome party until you were here for a week. A lot of people don't make it that long."

I gulped, wondering what she had done to them. I had been getting comfortable enough that I forgot she wasn't just any captain. She was Captain Tess the Terrible of the Daughters, ruthless enough that she was feared by the Saints. Did she kill those who didn't make the cut? Did she feed them to the sirens?

"What–" I started and stopped, building my courage back up before starting again, "What happens to them?"

I met her eye and was met with a confused look on her face. "We drop them at the next port we sail to if they don't want to be here or can't hack it on the seas."

I blinked. "That's–"

"Not what you were expecting?" Tess finished for me.

I nodded.

"You have to stop thinking like a Saint. Pirates aren't the devils you were taught to fear," Tess said.

She was right, of course. We were taught so much about the sirens, the sea devils, that I had been unlearning that I hadn't really thought about what I had learned about the pirates. As the defenders of the sirens, they were almost worse than the creatures themselves because they could have been holy and made the choice to turn their backs on the gods and court the devil.

I didn't know what I believed about the gods now, but I had seen firsthand that the sirens didn't hurt us. I didn't know if that made us hells blessed, but I did know that any god that blessed the Saints wasn't one I cared to impress.

"I'm sorry," I said slowly. "You've all been nothing but nice to me."

They all reassured me it was fine.

"The ideas they drill into you don't go away overnight," Neta said.

I wondered again what her story was and if it was similar to mine. She had the making and manners of a Convent brat, and I wondered if our paths had ever crossed.

"Hearing the stories helps," Scyla said. "I'll start." She paused a moment and asked, "How much do you remember from before the Saints?"

"Not much."

"I didn't think so. You're a bit younger than me, and I was just a kid when the White Robes swept in. Old enough to understand a bit, but too young to do anything about it. Now, people describe it as the intervention of the gods. I view it more as the intrusion of devils, but neither is quite right. Nothing changed overnight. They came bearing gifts and warnings of the horrors they had experienced at the hands of the seas. We didn't believe at first, of course. The Isles had always been friends of the sea. Most of us even worshipped the sea goddess Nema, who provided for us and ensured balance between the seas and the land. We used to have a summer festival in her honor."

"But Nemo's the god of the sea."

"Goddess. They weren't even creative in their rewrites," Scyla groaned before continuing. "Nemo wasn't a name known to us until the White Robes came. Before them, we had a whole host of different gods and goddesses."

"Goddesses?" I asked quietly.

Tess spoke up then. "Aye, there used to be more goddesses than gods. The goddesses were revered above the gods for their strength and abilities. Before the White Robes brought their false gods here, women were honored and treated as equals."

Addie moved to my side and put a hand on my shoulder. I blinked in surprise at her warm smile before reminding myself that, pirates or not, every one of these women was more caring and kinder than almost everyone in the Convent. "I know it's hard to believe, but if you think back, really think, the signs are there."

My confusion must have shown on my face, because she continued, "Have you ever wondered why the oldest books there seem to have all come from within our lifetime? Even in the Convent's library that's supposed to hold all the knowledge of the Isles from the past centuries, nothing on display is over twenty years old."

"They say everything else is kept under lock and key in the rare book room," I said slowly.

"A lie, and a poor one at that," Neta added.

Addie nodded quickly. "And all the oldest portraits and mosaics and statues of the gods were refreshed and changed. If you look at the redone paintings, it's clear they changed the faces and bodies of many of them. They changed our history to fit their own agenda. They vandalized our art and called it repair, but they missed a few. In the northwest chapel that rarely gets any use, there's a colored glass window of Nema that somehow survived, at least until I left."

I couldn't breathe through my shock. I knew that place. Of course I did. It was my favorite place in the Convent. Sketching under the rays of rainbow, basking in the light of the glass, was the only place in the Convent besides my own room that had felt safe.

I had been mesmerized by the siren, even if I didn't admit it to myself then. She was beautiful from the top of her raven hair to the tip of her emerald tail.

I knew the Saints liked to be dramatic in their teachings and had assumed the lesson was that sometimes evil came in a beautiful form and that beauty didn't equate to goodness, but that in and of itself had been surprising. Most of their teachings and stories talked about how beauty was to be aspired to and was a sign of godliness.

It hadn't made sense to me. That being the sea goddess made even less sense.

"I know the one, but that means that Nema, the sea goddess, is a–" I stopped, unable to say the last part. They waited for me to force out, "A siren?"

"Not exactly," Tess said quickly. "Do you want to explain, love?"

"Sure. So yes and no. To surface dwellers, she might be considered a siren, but below the seas, she's considered Mer, the Queen of the Mer."

"She's not following. Maybe back up a couple of steps," Scyla said gently. I shot her a grateful look since she was right, I wasn't following. *Was Mer another name for siren?*

Mel smiled at me, saying, "Apologies, I got ahead of myself. I don't often talk of my life before this ship, but I was, or rather, I am, a siren."

*Yeah, right.*

I looked around at the others, waiting for someone to crack a smile at her joke, but no one did. "You can't be serious."

"She is. Deadly serious. There's so much more to the seas than we knew. Mel's the reason we know as much as we do about the sirens and one of the reasons I would protect them with my life."

"You're a siren?" I asked looking at Mel. I was used to her strange looks by now, but it was hard to deny the evidence of her eyes. They looked more siren than human.

"Your eyes..." I said.

She nodded encouragingly.

"You said they were a gift from Nema."

Again she nodded.

"Nema the sea goddess? She changed your eyes?" I asked.

She laughed, "Not literally. Not in whatever way you're thinking. But yes, my eyes changed when I transformed from Mer to a siren."

I had so many questions, but the first thing to pop out of my mouth was, "You used to be a goddess?"

Her musical laugh rang out and she quickly said, "Seas, no. I'm not explaining this well. Nema the goddess of the sea is the Queen of the Mer. She's a goddess, closer to a siren than Mer, but she isn't quite either. The Mer aren't any more gods and goddess than you surface dwellers are."

"So Mer are another type of siren?" I asked slowly.

"Sort of," she said pausing a moment before adding, "it's more like sirens are another type of Mer. Mer can become sirens, but a siren can't become Mer. When a Mer undergoes the transition, they become stronger, faster, and more dangerous. It's why surface dwellers don't see Mer. They're too vulnerable to be that close to the surface."

I had so many questions, but I couldn't move past the obvious. Sure, she looked unusual, but she still looked human. "But–"

I stopped myself, wondering how rude it would be to ask how she had legs.

She smiled. "It's alright, I'm sure you have questions."

"You have legs," I said in wonder.

"Not a question," she said, still grinning.

"Do all sirens secretly have legs?"

"If they're out of water for long enough."

"Could you turn back if you wanted?"

"I could, but I don't."

"We don't really talk about that," Addie said softly.

"It's okay, you don't have to explain," I said quickly, sensing her discomfort and not wanting to continue to cause it.

"It's okay. It's my origin story after all. The short version is that I was trapped on a ship for a long time with those monsters until Tess, here, came and rescued me. I haven't transformed in a long time. I worry what the siren in me might do. I was kept prisoner for a long time and I–" she took a deep breath, her hands shaking.

"And I don't want her taking any risks," Tess finished for her. "I don't want her anywhere near the ship of men who hurt her. I couldn't stand to lose you," she said to Mel softly.

"It's not a sign of weakness to be cautious. It's a sign of strength," Addie added.

"They didn't see her as human," Scyla explained softly to me, before continuing louder, "She had it the worst of us all. Compared to Melody, my story's pretty tame. I was offshore fishing when a storm swooped in out of nowhere. I tried to row back, but the wind and waves took me out to open sea. A nasty wave hit the boat and capsized it. I hit my head hard before sinking. The last thing I remember was the icy cold of the water before I lost consciousness. When I came to, I was safely on shore, lying on the beach. I slowly sat up and saw her, a siren resting there on the rocks. She grinned when she saw me notice her, blew me a kiss, and dove into the water. With a wave of her tail, she was gone. I knew without question that she had saved my life. Now, my family were fishermen, but even they had been listening to the teachings of the Saints, so they didn't believe me. They said it was blasphemous to thank the devils for something the gods did. I learned to stop talking about it, but I didn't let it go. Tess was the first person I heard say anything not negative about the sirens." Scyla and Tess grinned at each other before Scyla turned back to me and said, "I took a chance and told her my story, and she offered me a way out, a new life, and a way to repay my debt to the sea. I jumped at it and never looked back."

I was in awe. "A siren saved you?"

She nodded. "She did, and then Tess did. I was slowly dying in that village. We were still holding on to some of our beliefs, but the men were already starting to act superior to us. Boys that I used to call friends were degrading to me because they felt they could. On the bad days, I miss my family, but I wouldn't trade what I have here for the world. I have a new family now," she said, grinning at the room, before pulling me into a bone-crushing hug. "And it just got a bit bigger."

Addie spoke up. "I'm a Convent brat," she said. Scyla let go of me and I watched in disbelief as Addie rolled up her sleeve, knowing what I would see when she did because I had my own matching one on my shoulder. I wanted to look away, but I wouldn't disrespect her like that. Her sleeve revealed swirls of ink that I knew were the bottom of an anchor. Except when she fully revealed the image, it was altered. I gasped and hurried toward her. I reached out a hand to touch the image before it even occurred to me to pause.

She smiled, "It's okay, you can touch it."

I gently touched the anchor, tracing the familiar swirls, but hers had been altered. Wrapped around the anchor's arm was the tail of a beautiful siren, who was sitting on the anchor. "It's beautiful."

She grinned, "Thanks, but it was Tess's idea."

Tess shrugged. "I hated seeing the girls come in marked by something they didn't choose. Flora figured out how to alter them. She thinks she can remove the markings as well, but surprisingly, no one has asked her to try."

It wasn't surprising to me at all. The anchor was a part of my story, ever since I was thirteen when the Convent deemed me old enough and of value to be marked. It told a tale of my perseverance and strength. It marked me as a Convent brat, a survivor. I didn't want it removed, but I wouldn't mind having it altered.

"Would I be able to get something like that done?" I asked, rolling up my sleeve and looking at my own anchor, identical to Addie's but without the siren wrapped around the Saint's symbol. Now that I had seen the beauty of what it could be, I wanted it.

"Of course," Tess said. "Flora can do whatever you want to it, but a lot of people choose a siren. It's become a symbol for our crew. Most who see that symbol know we're the Daughters of the Deep, the resistance standing against the heretics and their goal of siren genocide. It's a symbol of hope, but of course, it also strikes fear into the hearts of the heretics. That's a fun bonus."

"Neta has one too," Addie said, nodding in her direction.

Neta showed me a flash of hers and said, "The White Robes took my sister. We had been fighting the night they took her. The last words I said to her were in anger. I waited around for a few weeks, hoping she would come back, but part of me knew it was already too late. When they told me she was called to the sea, I made my escape."

That seemed to be all she was going to say on the matter, and I wasn't sure what I should or shouldn't ask. That was more than I had ever heard Neta speak in one go, and I didn't want to say the wrong thing and ruin it.

When the silence continued to linger, Addie stepped in and said, "Thankfully, I found her before any of the guards did."

Neta rolled her eyes at that. "Please, they wouldn't have found me."

I was inclined to believe her. She was incredibly skilled at hiding in the shadows. It was a necessary survival skill a lot of us on the ship, myself included, had learned to master in the Convent, but Neta was far more skilled than most. She blended incredibly well and was easily overlooked when she wanted to be.

"How did you get here?" I asked Addie, knowing Neta didn't want to share anymore.

Addie took a deep breath and clasped her hands together. She was playing with a silver ring on her finger. I gave her a minute before saying, "You don't have to if you don't want to." They didn't owe me their stories, but I would gratefully listen to anything they were willing to share. So much about life in the Convent had never made sense to me, but I'd never had anyone to ask. The Saints and even the other women got angry when I asked my questions, and I eventually grew old enough to know not to ask.

She smiled softly. "That's alright, it's hard to think about, especially knowing what I do now. They took a friend of mine," she said simply.

I waited, and Tess gave her a sympathetic smile. Scyla looked like she was about to jump in and say something, but Addie kept going. "Actually, that's a bit of a lie. We weren't really friends. I don't know how to describe what we were. We grew up together on one of the outer Isles. She was always there for me when it mattered, but we argued constantly. We were incredibly competitive and, seas, I hated it when she beat me at anything."

There was a faraway look in her eye when she continued, "We were foolish back then, but so were our people. When the Saints came, our people changed. They had always been peaceful and kind, but the Saints changed that. At the time I thought the fear of the sirens caused the change, but now I know it was the Saints. Our people turned into monsters, still human, but without any compassion. When the Saints decided to take me, her, and some other girls away from the island, it seemed like a blessing."

"They love to look like saviors," Scyla added.

"They sure do, and we believed it too. We were so thankful to be rescued from our island that we accepted their ideas without question."

Her shoulders slumped a little, but she continued, "They were supposed to take me, but they took my friend instead. When she found out I was picked to bless a cleansing mission, she saw that as the ultimate loss. She took it as the Convent siding with me, picking me over her. I don't know what she did, nor would I like to, but somehow, with less than a day before the mission, she convinced one of the more powerful Saints to change their minds. They took her instead, a betrayal that I was livid about at the time, especially since she left bragging. But she—" Addie paused, looking down at her ring, spinning it around her finger. "She, um—she never came back."

She sighed and gave a pained smile. "Whether she knew it or not, she saved me. Since then, I've been racked with guilt and promised myself that I would find out what the Saints were up to and what really happened on those trips and, if possible, put a stop to it. Luckily, before I could really get myself into trouble, I found Tess defacing one of their temples. I told her my story and she took me in."

"We know a little more than we used to about the Saints and the sirens themselves thanks to Mel, but not nearly enough to pose as much of a threat as I would like unfortunately," Tess said with resignation in her voice that pained me.

Scyla looked at me and then back at Tess. "You know she's too polite to ask, Cap."

Tess chuckled. "Fine, fine. I know you lot must be sick of my story, but it's time. I was supposed to be the Saint's first sacrifice."

I gasped at that. Yes, I knew they weren't good men, but this confirmed my worst suspicions and fears. "They were going to sacrifice you?"

"They tried, but even back then, I had more determination and courage than the lot of them."

I thought for a moment before gasping again. "But... but... back then, you couldn't have been more than-"

"Ten. I was ten years old when they took me, determined to give my life to their gods in exchange for control of the Isles. I'm not sure where they were taking me, but thankfully, they didn't make it there. The ship was attacked, and I was washed overboard in the struggle into the waiting arms of what looked like Nema herself. It was probably just a siren, but I felt safe for the first time since the Saints had come, for the first time since my mother disappeared. The siren rescued me and brought me to a fisherman who got me to the mainland. I was on my own there, but at least I was safe."

Her dedication to the sirens made more sense now. She felt like she owed them her life since they had rescued her and gifted her a new life.

"I travelled for a while. I was lucky enough that most of the people I met were helpful. I trained on the mainland, in Altea, dreaming about the day I would come back and help my–" She paused and amended, "Our people. When I was older and strong enough, I started collecting lost souls like me."

Shortly after that, we called it a night, but I lay awake in my hammock, thinking about everything I had learned, especially about Tess's story.

Tess treated it like it was no big deal what she did, but it was everything to so many of us. Like all of us on the ship, my life had been touched by the sirens, of course, but they hadn't been my rescuers.

Tess took her life into her own hands and did everything she could to help others like herself, like me. She sought out those the Saints of Santerra hadn't sunk their ideals and beliefs into and those who had lost loved ones to the call of the sea. She gave us hope and the chance to change things, to fight back against the heretics that would rather see us all as dead sirens than as strong women.

She rescued us and gave us the only chance we had of seeing our loved ones again.

Tess believed they were still out there as sirens, and if Mel was anything to go by, they hadn't lost everything they were. Cora might still be out there somewhere in the body of a siren. While there was that hope, I would sail the seas until I found her, or until the sea called me to join her.

I had made her a promise: I would love her until the seas claimed me and even after, and by sin or by sail, I would find her.

# CHAPTER TWENTY
# Ray

I narrowed my eyes as the same Saints' ship sailed by us again. Rage boiled in my blood as they taunted us. They weren't doing anything, but their proximity was enough to drive me to anger.

This wasn't the first time they had sailed past us, but Tess still didn't let us attack. She insisted that we spare the innocent, that otherwise we were no better than them, so things hadn't come to blows with the ship yet. We hadn't been able to catch them in the act of stalking sirens, but it was only a matter of time.

I knew the ship, though–knew the men who operated it. It was the same ship that had taken Cora, the same men that claimed she must have been "unholy" since the sea called her. Funny how the sea waited until they had their hands on her to claim her. Funny how the sea spared her all those nights she was by my side, but one night away and the sea came to call. It would be funny to watch them drown, to watch them be fed on by the very sirens they hunted. Too bad we didn't have enough proof yet.

I had pleaded with the captain after the first time they crossed our path, but she insisted. Even now, she held firm. Without proof, we couldn't draw first blood.

She didn't understand that even if what they were doing now was innocent, these men were anything but.

Unfortunately, they were careful. It was like they knew we were watching, waiting for a slip-up, waiting to attack. We saw the nets, the harpoons. To me, it was enough. I knew these sorts of men, and these men in particular. I didn't want to wait, but Tess still insisted. Rationally, I understood why, but the rage that filled me with every sight of their ship was hard to contain.

I had dreamed of boarding their ship and extracting the truth about Cora's disappearance with countless strokes of my dagger. I could feel it in my bones that they had made her bleed, and that could only be paid for in blood. I would torture the details out of each of them before throwing them to the sea to the very sirens they reviled.

I hadn't had a violent streak before they took her from me, but now violence coated my mind like a poison, caressed it like a lover. Rage consumed me when I thought of how she was ripped from me, of what she might be suffering without me to protect her, what hell she might be experiencing if she even still lived. There was no amount of blood that could repay that crime, but I would run their veins dry trying if given the chance.

It wasn't until Tess caught me crying in my hammock that she got it out of me why this ship mattered. I hadn't told her that I recognized it. She had already said no, and I hadn't thought it would matter. I was wrong.

She started preparing immediately, and the very next night, we started a hunt of our own.

# CHAPTER TWENTY ONE
## Ray

We stalked their ship for days to no avail. There wasn't a single siren sighting or any proof of any distressed women on the ship. There didn't appear to be any women on the ship at all. It was possible they were being kept below deck, but I hoped that wasn't the case.

I was growing weary of the waiting. I couldn't stand by knowing they could be hurting sirens or other women. After pacing the length of the ship more times than I could count, waiting for something to happen, I finally gave in and strode into Tess's office.

She was pouring over some maps on her large desk when I entered. She sighed and turned to me, "Any news?"

"No, nothing, and we've been watching for days. Can't we do something? If we wait for them to make a move, we might be too late."

"And what if they aren't the same men you know? What if the ship was sold to others? What if they might have the same mission we do?"

"There's not a chance in the hells that they're out here protecting anyone, not with all those nets and harpoons."

Tess looked at me and raised her eyebrows, gesturing to our ship. I followed her gaze and couldn't avoid seeing our cannons, harpoons, and giant nets.

"That's different."

She sighed. "I know you think you know these men, and I know you know the ship, but without proof, we can't attack them. If you knew without a doubt that the men in question were on board that ship, then we could make a move, but for now, we have to be patient. If you're right about them, they'll slip up, eventually."

That sparked an idea, a terrible, dangerous idea. One that might result in my death, but I couldn't bring myself to care, not when death's embrace might reunite me with her. "What if I can prove it?"

She looked at me with interest. "And how do you propose doing that?"

She wasn't going to like it; I knew that before I even said it.

"Well, I could board their ship—"

"No." She left no room for discussion with the force of her declaration, but I continued anyway.

"Tess, please hear me out, if I board their ship—"

"If you board their ship and they are the monsters you say, then who knows what they might do to you? It's not worth the risk."

"I know the risks, and I know those men. If they aren't stopped, who knows how many other women they'll hurt before we catch them."

She sighed, "I understand your frustration, but we have rules for a reason. Otherwise, we're no better than they are."

"And if we sit back and do nothing, we might be just as bad."

She scowled, groaning in frustration. "You're asking too much of me."

"And you of me. To sit here idly while those men that hurt Cora, those men that put their hands on her, those men that may as well have murdered her, sail free, is asking too much. Tess, please, what if it were Mel that had been taken?"

"Enough!" she ground out. "I'll hear no more of this. You haven't been with us long, so I've been lenient, but if you don't like my rules, you don't have to sail with us."

I gulped, instantly quiet, fighting my temper that wanted to flare out. My control was the one good thing that came from my years in the Convent. Regardless of how I was feeling, I knew how to hold my tongue.

I saw how conflicted and upset she looked and knew it pained her to have to tell me no, but knowing that did nothing for my temper, nothing for the fact that despite knowing how important this was to me, despite knowing the stakes, she still said no.

I wouldn't continue to argue. I couldn't, and she knew that. She might not know how bad my specific situation was and how hard it had been to make my escape from the Convent, but she should have some idea.

The Isles didn't let people walk away easily, the Saints even less so. The lengths I went to in order to escape ensured there was nowhere safe for me on the Isles, at least not without her crew.

I could try to find my way to the Zanarian mainland, but there was no guarantee that without the protection of the Daughters of the Deep, I would make it there unharmed. No guarantee that I would make it there at all.

Tess the Terrible was feared on these waters. Most of the hunters and other ships steered clear of us. It was a hard won honor and privilege.

Without her, I was nothing.

Without them, I had nothing.

I knew that, and she should, too. For her to threaten my place here over an argument, a disagreement, pissed me off.

I turned and stormed out of her office, not waiting to see if she had anything else to say. She had said enough. She was a hypocrite. There was no way that if Mel had been taken, if she had been hurt by those men masquerading as holy, that Tess would have stood down the way she was asking me to.

She valued my life more highly than I did. But I wasn't the defenseless little girl I used to be. I could handle myself if I was careful.

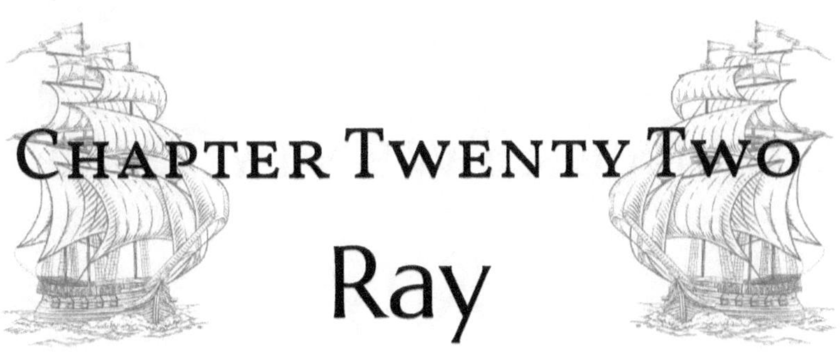

# Chapter Twenty Two
## Ray

I had held onto the hope that Cora might still be out there somewhere, but it hadn't gotten me anywhere, and the men that hurt her were likely on that ship, living and breathing, enjoying themselves. It was too much to stand.

I paced around the deck, still seeing red. How did Tess, knowing everything she did, honestly expect me to stand down?

I was willing to bet my life on the fact that that was Captain Butcher's ship, the last place Cora had been seen. The stories about him alone should have been enough to make Tess break her rule against attacking without proof. Never mind that he was the one that had taken Cora from me, he was one of the best siren hunters on the seas, and if the stories were to be believed, he didn't just kill them. He maimed and tortured the devil out of them until death came for them. It was despicable.

Now that Cora was gone, it was clear he didn't stop his abuse at sirens. I couldn't just stand by and wait for them to do it again. I couldn't stand by while they might be harming another being, siren or woman. I wouldn't do it.

I knew what I had to do, and there was no stopping me. If I made it back alive and was ousted from the crew, I would have to deal with that, but it would be worth it. Come hells or high water, the Saints were going to pay tonight.

# Chapter Twenty Three
## Ray

When the skies were dark, I donned my dagger that Scyla had gifted me that first night. I looked longingly at my sword, but knew I had to leave it in favor of traveling light.

I hadn't yet figured out how to make my way to the other ship. I didn't know if I could cut loose a rowboat without anyone noticing.

Scyla had been teaching me how to row better since my first attempt, and I was almost confident I would be able to do it on my own. Confident enough to try, at least. It was preferable to surrendering myself to the deep and praying that whatever might be lurking under the water would let me live long enough to swim the distance.

I knew that my best chance was to take a boat, so I just had to find a way to do so without it being missed.

I strolled the ship, doing a perimeter, trying to look as casual as possible, nodding to a few of the crew. They had become more of a family to me than I had ever experienced, and I hoped that however tonight went down, they wouldn't hate me for this.

I leaned over the edge, looking for the nearest rowboat, and saw what I was looking for. Quickly and quietly, I unsheathed my dagger and leaned over.

"Going somewhere?"

I jumped and yelped when I almost lost my grip on my dagger. Besides Cora's locket, it was my most prized possession. I caught it just in time and narrowly managed to avoid slicing my palm open.

Having it safely in hand, I turned around and saw Scyla standing there, watching me with an amused expression that dropped the moment she saw my face. "What's wrong?"

"Nothing," I said, but she knew better and just continued to stare at me, waiting. "Okay, fine. I was going to borrow the rowboat and pay a little visit to our holy friends over there."

She looked at me, evaluating. "And do what, exactly?"

I watched her, trying to decide how much to reveal. She already knew me too well to buy any sort of lie, and this was Scyla. I owed her the truth.

"The men that took the love of my life from me are on that ship, and I intend to make them pay. I intend to make the ocean run red with the blood of those so-called holy men who hurt her."

She looked around, and over her shoulder for any listening ears but didn't find any. It was just us. When she turned back, she grinned. "I knew I liked you. You're definitely keeping things interesting. How do you intend to get back here?"

I shrugged. "I didn't plan that far."

Her face became serious. "I'll only ask once. Are you sure this is worth it?"

I nodded. I didn't have to think twice about that. If the price for revenge was my life, I would pay it.

She looked around again. "Alright, but you promise me you'll fight like hells. I won't help with a suicide mission."

I nodded quickly, surprised and confused.

With that, she moved closer. "Well, what are you waiting for? We have to hurry. I might be the only one crazy enough to let you do this. Hurry up and jump."

Worried she might change her mind, I quickly hurled myself over the side and into the boat. She loosened the ropes, and I started my descent, watching her the entire time, worried she would change her mind, prepared to cut myself loose if she started to pull the boat back up. When the boat hit the water. I saluted her in thanks and picked up the oars to start rowing.

Fear shot through me when I heard a splash. A big one. I gulped. Yes, sirens weren't the enemy, but I had never been this close to them before. In this little boat, I was as good as chum for the sirens, or shark bait. I was ripe for the taking. I started desperately trying to row hard until I heard, "Hey, slow down, would you?"

I turned around and was shocked to find Scyla swimming her way over to me.

"What are you doing?"

"You didn't think I'd let you have all the fun yourself, did you?"

"You can't come with me."

She pulled herself up into the boat. She was soaking wet from head to toe. She gathered up her now dripping locs, unlaced the ribbon from her tunic and tied them back. "This shit is gonna take forever to dry. You're lucky I like you."

With that, she grabbed one of the oars from me and started to row.

"I'm serious! You can't be here. It's too dangerous!"

She rolled her eyes. "It would've been with just you. I'm here now though, and I can promise you, we won't be the ones who end up dead."

As grateful as I was to her for volunteering, and as valuable as her help would be, I didn't want this. I didn't want her blood on my hands. "You can't. I can't ask you to."

"Lucky for us, I didn't wait for you to ask, and I won't take no for an answer. Now shut up and start rowing."

She was right. We were wasting time and going sideways since I hadn't started helping her row. It was only a matter of time until the crew noticed we were missing or until the other ship noticed something in the water. We had to hurry.

She grinned at me, knowing she had won, and we started to row hard and fast in tandem. I had to admit, it was much easier with her along for the ride.

Thankfully, both ships had pulled in their sails for the night. Otherwise, we would've had a rough go of it, but as it was, it was smooth sailing.

When we reached the ship, we surveyed the area, looking for the best way to board. It wasn't long before we found what we needed: a rope.

Since my escape from the Saints, I had spent hours learning to climb up and down ropes. I didn't want to be trapped anywhere again. Besides, on the sea, knowing how to climb could very much mean life or death.

I nodded to it, and Scyla's eyes lit up. "They're making this too easy. I mean, if they didn't want to be boarded, why give us an entry?"

She was right. It was sloppy, which gave me pause.

"You don't think it's a little too easy?" I asked.

"What do you mean?"

"Do you think it's a trap?"

She shrugged, "Could be. Does it change anything?"

I thought about it for a moment before I felt my resolve turn to steel. "No. I'll bring as many of them down with me as I can, even if it's a trap, but I'm doing this. I need to."

She nodded, understanding flashing over her face that had me imme-diately saying, "But it should change things for you. You don't have to do this. You can still leave."

She shook her head. "Not how that works. You're a Daughter now, and we always have each other's backs."

"But Tess–"

"Tess is our fearless leader, but sometimes when you're in charge of so many, the needs of the one get lost. She's right that this is impulsive and reckless, and it's her job to try to keep her crew intact and safe as much as possible."

"And as her first mate, what's your job?"

She grinned. "My job is to make sure she doesn't get too bogged down in our safety that she forgets about our mission. My job is to make sure we send the Saints back to their gods."

"You really, really should go back."

"And leave you to die? Absolutely not. I found you. That makes you my responsibility, and if I'm here, you'll think twice about throwing away your life."

"I'm not trying to throw away my life," I argued.

"You don't value it the way you value others' lives, so I'm staying, if only to make sure you fight. Really fight." She exhaled before adding, "I know how important this is to you. Trust me, I get it, but your girl wouldn't want you getting yourself killed for her. Kill *for* her all you want, but don't get killed in the process."

Her words felt like a stab to my heart, but she was right. The last thing Cora would want was me getting myself killed for her. I wasn't even sure if she would want me to avenge her. She was incredibly kind and forgiving.

I pushed the thought out of my mind. She wasn't here anymore because of these men. She wasn't here to make me a better person, and they were going to feel my pain.

"I'll be as careful as I can be."

Scyla put her oar down and gave me a small smile. "That's all I ask. So, what's the plan?"

I shrugged. "Get up there, kill their captain and as many of them as we can take down in the process, and get out alive?"

"So, we're winging it? Great."

I rolled my eyes. "If you have a better plan, I'm all ears."

She chuckled. "Hey, this is your mission. I'm just along for the ride."

"I really wish you weren't."

"Well, it's a good thing I don't care. Now, get climbing."

I pulled on the rope, testing it. Thankfully, it held. I looked back at Scyla. "Last chance. You sure I can't talk you into manning my escape boat?"

"And miss the action now that something exciting is finally happening around here? Not a chance."

As worried as I was for her, I had to admit I didn't hate that I wasn't going into this alone.

I pulled myself up onto the rope and started the climb. The rope jerked below me a few moments later when Scyla started her ascent.

We made quick work of the climb until we were almost at the top and I slowed, listening. I felt Scyla stop behind me.

"I don't hear anything," I whispered to her.

"That's not suspicious at all," she whispered back, voice laced with sarcasm.

It was ominous.

I couldn't hear *any* noise coming from the ship.

Yes, they were anchored, but still, there should be sounds of life from the deck.

"You sure you want to wander into this trap?" she whispered up at me.

I was sure. I was sure I didn't want her to get hurt, but I was even more sure that this was something I had to do. I needed to do this, partly for Cora, but mostly for me. I hadn't been able to save Cora. I hadn't been able to help her while she was here. I felt so helpless and I was sick of it. This was at least something I could do. If I couldn't save Cora, I could at least stop them from hurting others. Yes, there would always be men like them out there, but these men weren't going to continue to hurt women if I had anything to say about it.

# Chapter Twenty Four
## Coral

My sisters and I were on the move again when I felt a tug in my gut. I couldn't tell what it was, but something was telling me that I was swimming away from where I needed to be.

*There's something I need to take a look at,* I thought in my pod's direction before turning around.

I felt a hand on my shoulder and turned around. Charia looked concerned. *What is it?*

*I don't know, but something is telling me I need to be going this way.*

*Is there danger? I don't sense any distress.*

I didn't either—not distress at least, just a strong feeling that I was too curious not to follow.

*I don't know.*

*We're coming,* Charia thought.

*You don't have to.*

*But we will. Sisters don't let sisters swim into the unknown alone.*

I grinned at her and the rest of the pod over her shoulder. They grinned back.

*Maybe it'll be worth our while,* Sypher thought. *It's been a while since we've seen any action.*

Despite what she said, I knew I wasn't alone in being happy that we hadn't had any incidents in a little while. Every time we tangled tails with the hunters, we risked our lives. While it was rewarding to see the life drain out of their eyes, it wasn't worth losing another sister. Our latest addition hadn't been with us for more than a few weeks before she was killed in battle by the hunters.

It was heartbreaking for everyone, but especially for Ostoma, who had spent the entire few weeks healing her and teaching her our ways. The losses were always the hardest on her, but none of us took it lightly.

We had been more careful afterward, and I didn't want to risk our safety now, but I knew I couldn't ignore this feeling.

I kept going, and my sisters turned tails and swam in behind me. I knew they would have my back, but it felt nice to have family I could count on.

As we kept going, I started to worry. I wasn't even sure what we were looking for, but I hoped I would know it when I saw it.

I just had to hope that whatever I was sensing wasn't pulling us right into a trap.

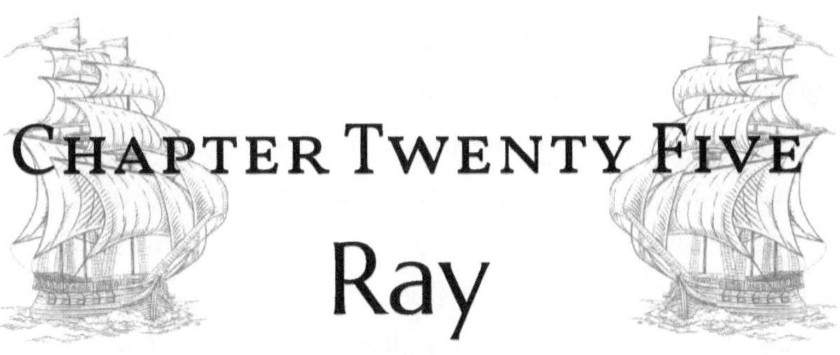

# Chapter Twenty Five
## Ray

The deck was as deserted as it sounded. Scyla and I were careful to stick to the shadows, but there wasn't anyone around to see us anyway.

I gestured to the door leading down below the deck, and Scyla nodded grimly. We both knew this wasn't a good sign. We must be interrupting something important if they had all deserted the deck.

I carefully inched open the door, and we heard ceremonial music coming from below. Voices drifted in our direction, and I ducked into the first door I found, pulling Scyla in behind me, hoping the gods were on our side and the room was empty.

The second she was in, I shut the door as quietly as I could manage. I breathed out a sigh of relief when I looked around and saw we were alone. We were in some sort of storage closet that seemed to hold a ship's worth of spare Saints' robes. The gods were looking out for us. Scyla grabbed one and tossed me another.

"Pretty lucky, huh?"

"Extremely. They won't see us coming until it's too late," I said, pulling the robe over my head. It was long enough to cover everything but my black boots. Not perfect since the Saints only wore white shoes, but it was better than nothing.

"So, what's the plan? Now that you're not going down with the ship, is this a 'deal as much damage as possible' mission or a stealth strike mission?"

"Huh?" I had been with the Daughters long enough now that I usually knew what they were talking about, but not this time.

"Are we trying to kill as many people as we can, or do we have a target?"

I had been intending to do as much damage as possible back when I didn't plan on making it back to the Daughters, but with Scyla here, I was going to have to be more careful.

I wasn't going to be able to take all of them out myself anyway, even with Scyla's help. It was too big a job for us. We could've managed it with the rest of the crew, but they weren't here, and Tess wasn't willing to budge on the issue.

My mind froze on the thought as it occurred to me. "Maybe we bring Tess some proof?" I asked, thinking out loud.

"Meaning?"

"We check the ship for ourselves and find something proving they're hunters. Cap would have to do something about it then, right?"

Scyla broke into a grin. "Now you're thinking. Of course, Tess'll kill us if we make it out of here without something good, so we better find something."

After a quick debate, we split up.

I headed to where the Captain's quarters should be, and Scyla headed down toward the music. I had argued with her, of course, but she insisted that since it was my mission, I should be the one to ransack the Captain's quarters. She insisted it was the more dangerous task.

I foolishly listened.

I was busy looking for anything useful in the Captain's quarters when I heard her scream.

# CHAPTER TWENTY SIX
# Coral

The pod followed right behind me, and it wasn't long before Charia spoke up. *You were right.*

*You feel it too?*

*Of course, same as always. Someone's in trouble.*

I was glad that following my instincts had paid off, but I wasn't sure that was exactly the pull I had been feeling.

We swam further, and then I felt it. The pull that said we were needed, that someone needed us.

Sypher was getting her wish after all – we were going to see some action.

*Faster,* Charia said to everyone. *The feeling is growing.*

# Chapter Twenty Seven
## Ray

*Scyla.*

I dropped the papers I was holding, reached under my robe, and palmed my dagger. Thankfully, I remembered to pause a moment and flip up my hood. I was going to kill them if they hurt her, but it would be easier if I weren't seen yet.

Before I could take my first step toward the door, it opened. In strolled Father Alaric, and it wasn't hard to guess from his swagger that he had been gifted more responsibility around the ship since I had eliminated his competition. Garrick used to be Captain Butcher's second, and it looked like the Captain hadn't wasted any time doling out a promotion.

"Ledair," he barked out. "What in the hells are you still doing up here? Didn't you hear me?"

I straightened, wondering who Ledair was. I risked shaking my head, not wanting to speak.

He groaned, throwing his head back. "Some guard you are." He turned on his heel and left. I was frozen to the spot, and before I could even think about making another move, he ducked back in, growling at me.

"Useless little wretch, get your ass out here. We don't have time to waste. The moon is just right, and we caught a stowaway who'll be perfect for a ritual."

Scyla.

I fell quickly into step behind him, keeping my head down, hoping it would be enough to hold my hood in place. I needed every bit of luck I could get.

What in the hells were they planning to do with her? I would fight like hells for her, but I knew without a doubt that if I survived tonight, the Daughters, especially Captain Tess, might never forgive me for putting Scyla in danger.

Even if we both survived, my life as I knew it was over. I might have even forfeited my spot on the crew, and all because I couldn't do the one thing Tess had asked and stay patient. It had made sense at the time, but now I couldn't help wondering how I had been so stupid. I really hoped Scyla wasn't about to pay for my stupidity with her life.

# Chapter Twenty Eight
## Coral

As we grew closer, the two feelings warred inside of me, the feeling of rightness and the feeling of pain, of panic.

Charia stopped short in front of me, and I barely avoided colliding with her back. Coming to a stop, I was able to see what she saw.

*There are two ships.*

*Which one's our target?* Lucia asked.

Charia turned to me. *Which do you feel drawn to?*

I paused a moment, swimming a little closer, when a wave of panic hit me. It was more concentrated on the left. There were more people there feeling it. On the right, there was a lethal dose of terror and panic, but also the feeling of peace I had been following.

*That one,* I said, pointing to the right.

Leader grinned. *I knew you had it in you, little one. The more panic coming from a ship, the less likely they are to be our true target. The ships we want are those with a lone feeling of panic among a sea of glee.*

I nodded like I understood, but glee wasn't what I felt. It was rightness, peace, calm, and knowing it was coming from our target made it feel all the more wrong.

*Sypher and Lucia, you take the right. Coral, you're with me.*

Pride rushed through me at that. Fighting by her side was an honor. I grinned as I swam up to flank her.

*Alright, sisters, let's show them the real meaning of power.*

We swam closer, and I felt my sisters' glee increase as we took in the second ship we were passing.

*It's our allies!*

*The pirates!*

*I hope they're alright,* Rezi added.

I wondered if helping our pirate allies was what had called me here, but I still wasn't sure. The only thing I knew was that the feeling I had followed wasn't coming from their ship.

Our target loomed into view, and it became glaringly obvious why I was here. This was the very same ship that sent me to the seas in the first place.

*It's them.* No wonder coming after them had felt so right. Revenge would bring me peace.

I felt my sisters give into their sirens now that the hunt was on, but I still felt clear-minded. I wondered if it had something to do with the feeling that drew me here. The seas were looking out for me. They knew this wasn't going to be easy.

As glad as I was to finally have a shot at the scum who sold me to the sea, the timing wasn't ideal. For one, the girl on the ship needed rescuing, and our allies being as close as they were to the hunters was sure to spell trouble. Those complications weren't insurmountable, of course, but the ship itself posed a problem. It was huge, way larger than the ships we normally faced, and likely more deadly.

If we could take our time with the ship, I knew we could bring it down safely, but with the girl at risk and our allies so close, I wasn't sure time was a luxury we would have.

A moment later, Charia stopped at my side and nodded grimly. I wasn't sure how many of my thoughts she had heard, but it was clear she agreed.

*Ready sisters?* Charia asked as we glided into place. *This is going to go quickly.* She shot a look at me as she reminded us, *Our top priority is the girl on that ship.* Even as she said that, we could feel her need for help increasing. *She's our top priority, followed closely by helping the pirates, and then by destroying the ship.*

The pirates ranking above the destruction of the ship was disappointing but not surprising. Charia often reminded us about the importance of protecting our own, and for a reason I didn't understand and hadn't dared to ask, she claimed the pirates as her own.

She looked at me again and said in a way I knew was just meant for me, *If they get away, I promise you, we will find them again. You will have your revenge, even if it isn't this night.*

*We'll do our best to bring them down,* Lucia added.

They were right, of course. The ship wouldn't escape me forever. I was a monster, and the hunters may not know it yet, but I had marked them as my prey, and come hells or high water, they wouldn't get away.

I nodded to Charia. I understood and wouldn't jeopardize the mission. Before she gave the signal, I closed my eyes and turned my thoughts inward, still finding it odd that my siren hadn't wrestled control from me at the first sign of the ship. I had never had to purposely give her control before. I let myself imagine the leash I kept her on and opened my imaginary hands.

When my eyes reopened, I was back to being a passenger in my body, but I found this time I didn't mind. My siren was ruthless, and these men deserved the revenge she was prepared to take out on their flesh.

# Chapter Twenty Nine
## Ray

Before we made it below deck, the ship rocked forcefully, almost knocking me off my feet.

It felt like a large wave knocking against the ship. It felt dangerous, like hope I shouldn't dare to have yet.

Alaric stupidly ran to the side, grabbing hold of the railing and looking down. His head shot up, and I saw the fear in his eyes as he yelled, "Warn the others! The devils are on us!"

Sirens. Thank the gods the sirens were here.

I turned and ran for the door that led down below.

"Hurry!" he yelled, running over to man one of the harpoons. I looked back once more as the ship rocked again, and blessed be the seas, he fell overboard, screaming the entire way down. I hoped there was a particularly hungry siren waiting down there for him.

I whipped open the door and rushed below the deck. I needed to get the men on deck as quickly as possible and get Scyla out of here.

When the first group of men looked up at me, I tried to make my voice deep as I said, "Alaric's gone overboard! He needs help!"

Some of them ran past me, and then the ship rocked again, and more men ran out, set on stabilizing the ship. I moved further, following the haunting melody of the ceremonial music I could still hear. If I had to kill everyone in that room to save Scyla, I would find a way.

I made it past a few other chambers with panicking men running out behind me, and finally, the music stopped. I was about to pull open the door to the ceremonial chamber when I heard the captain's bellowing voice through the door.

"It must be the sirens, men! Gear up! Be prepared! We're sending them back to hell tonight!"

I ducked out of sight around the corner as men started pouring out of the chamber. They scrambled for their weapons and gear, bumping into one another. It would've been a funny sight if it weren't for the reason. They weren't inherently clumsy, but they had all blocked their ears. No wonder the sirens weren't sinking as many ships. The Saints were evolving, which definitely complicated things.

As the last man rushed past my hiding spot, I ran to the door and yanked it open. The sight that met me was bone chilling.

Scyla was on the ground next to a blood-stained altar, and she wasn't moving. I rushed to her side.

She had a swollen eye and a bloody lip, but I couldn't see much else through the robe. I grabbed for the bottom to lift it gently, praying to the gods and the seas that she was still alive.

I almost screamed when she bolted upright and started swinging at me. I was so thankful she was alive, I pulled her to me, hugging her tight.

"What the hells are you doing?" she yelled out.

"It's me," I shushed her, pulling away and pulling down the hood so she could see me. She grinned when she saw my face.

I grinned back, unable to help myself. I was so lucky she was alive and even luckier she hadn't stabbed me.

"What are you doing here? Where did everyone go? I was just getting ready to give them hells."

"Sirens. Come on, we've gotta get out of here!"

She jumped to her feet, and I blinked in surprise when she held out her hand to help me up. "Hey, I'm doing the rescuing here," I said, taking her hand and letting her pull me to standing.

She laughed. "Sure you are. Now come on."

"Wait, some of them blocked their ears. They won't be under the sirens' spell."

She took that in stride, saying, "Well, better odds than I had a few minutes ago anyway, so I'll take it."

She pulled off her robe and grabbed a dagger in each hand.

"What are you doing?"

"They already know I'm here. Hiding doesn't do me any good." She paused a moment. "Wait, did you get what you came for?"

I shrugged, "I didn't find anything, but I'm sure Tess is going to give them hells for us when we make it back."

"When?" she repeated.

I nodded. When, not if. We weren't dying here if I had anything to say about it.

I started to pull off my own robe, but she shook her head. "Leave it, they know I'm here. You're still a fun surprise."

She was right that it was worth a shot. Maybe in the chaos, I could still pass for one of them.

"Alright, come on, we have to get out."

# Chapter Thirty
# Coral

They were firing at us, and we were doing everything we could, but even I knew we weren't going to be able to bring the ship down. Our allies were too worried about hurting the girl still on the ship to fight as ruthlessly as they would need to.

They had tried sending a few boats over, but the cannons and harpoons didn't let the pirates get close. We were doing everything we could to damage the ship from below, but it wasn't working as well as it should have. Neither were our powers. Half the ship should've been in our clutches by now, but there weren't many bodies in the water.

*Does someone have the girl?* Charia asked.

Everyone answered no, but we knew why she was asking. The panic was gone, which was either a really good or really bad sign. Either way, we knew we needed to keep up what we were doing.

# Chapter Thirty One
## Ray

We made it out onto the deck without incident, but the deck itself was in chaos with men running all over yelling out orders that no one else could hear and trying to restrain others who could hear the sirens from jumping overboard. I pushed Scyla in front of me and grabbed her arms from behind, trying to make it look like I was restraining her. I pulled her in the direction our boat should be waiting.

The others were largely too busy to notice us. There were a few wide eyes from the men who did see us, but no one had the time to stop and question me. It brought me some joy to see how scared they were of the sirens they were fighting.

Since they were attempting to rid the seas of sirens, they should be scared. Even over the noise of their cannons, I could hear the siren song. It was beautiful, of course, but it didn't affect us the same way it was affecting the men.

Women knew better. We knew beauty could be deadly and the promises of safety and love that they sang of were just pretty dreams. Their songs were beautiful, but I wasn't trying to throw myself overboard to be with them.

I skidded to a stop with Scyla where we had tied the rope to the boat. I grabbed around for it, finding nothing. My heart sank.

We were trapped.

Scyla turned around and asked, "Do you trust me?"

I nodded. "Of course."

"You're not going to like it."

"We don't have time for me to complain, so if you have a plan, tell me."

"We have to swim for it."

I blanched at that. I had come around to the idea of sirens not being as deadly to us as they were to men. I knew from the tales of the others that the sirens didn't consider us their enemies, but no matter how friendly I was told they were, I wasn't itching to go for a swim with them, especially in the middle of a battleground.

Our ship wasn't far, but I wasn't sure we could swim fast enough to get out of cannon range, and wasn't sure the sirens would be able to tell us from the enemy.

"Are you sure?" I asked.

"They won't hurt us. Besides, it's not like we have another choice. I can even go first. If they eat me, just don't follow," she said with a wink before pulling herself over the railing and tumbling off the ship.

I gasped and leaned over the railing, watching her go under. I started counting, reaching twenty before she reemerged, grinned and giving me a salute before she started swimming faster than I thought was humanly possible. It wasn't until I noticed the flick of the tail next to her that I realized she was being pulled. Thankfully, it was toward our ship.

I was about to follow her when I heard footsteps behind me. I whirled around and felt the wind take my hood. It was Captain Butcher. Seas, was I screwed. I was a competent fighter now, but I was no match for the butcher of the seas.

I saw the Captain's eyes widen in shock before narrowing, his hand moving to his sword. "What do we have here? Another stowaway?"

I mouthed nonsensical words at him, hoping he would be stupid enough to remove his plugs. At the same time, I was already trying to judge the distance between him and me and how quickly I could pull myself over the railing. I didn't think I could win in a fight, but I didn't need to win, just outlast him long enough to throw myself overboard. There was a chance I could do that.

He looked confused and went to reach for his ears. I really thought he might do it, but a moment later, his hands dropped, and he glared at me.

"You can't truly believe I would be that stupid."

From the look on his face, I knew I had messed up. I should've thrown myself overboard the second he emerged. Turning around to face him had been a mistake that might prove fatal. He would skewer me in the time it took me to swing myself over the railing. Flight wasn't an option, and from his face, it was clear the time for talking was over, too.

I shrugged for his benefit, mumbling to myself, "Can't blame a girl for trying."

I quickly reached under my robe and grabbed my dagger, straightening up just in time to meet his steel with mine. The force of his blow had me taking an involuntary step back.

I was starting to panic, but tried to remind myself I didn't need to win. I just needed him hurt or distracted long enough for me to get off the ship.

As hard as I had trained, I knew I was no match for Captain Butcher. His name was pronounced Boo-shay, but his reputation for slaughter had everyone calling him Captain Butcher, or the butcher of the seas. I had to get myself overboard, and quickly before he gutted me like a fish.

I parried another blow and jumped back, avoiding the next. I braced myself against the rail, hoping for a moment's reprieve to drag myself up. Unfortunately, distractions were hard to come by when your opponent couldn't hear. I ducked his next blow, hoping his momentum might carry him over, but unfortunately, he remained on deck and didn't appear to be tiring.

I was going to have to end this before he ended me.

He swung again and again. My dagger was there to meet his every blow, but this time, I stomped down hard on his toes. He flailed out, his sword launching my dagger back and away from me as he hopped back on his good foot. He lost his balance and fell back to the ground. I took that as my sign that I had overstayed my welcome, and without turning my back to him, I hoisted myself up onto the ledge. I wasn't focused enough, already worrying about the sirens in the sea below, and didn't notice until it was too late that the Captain's grimace had turned into a grin.

My only warning was the glint of steel before it came hurtling toward me. I looked down in shock, crying out as pain and panic flashed through me at the sight of my own dagger buried to the hilt in my stomach.

Then I fell.

# Chapter Thirty Two
## Coral

The feeling had been largely quiet when the fight started. My sisters and I were busy trying to make sure the pirates stayed alive and afloat and that the hunters didn't. I had let the siren take control until I felt that feeling again.

I was under the far end of the ship with Charia trying to tilt the ship and send men overboard, but the feeling took my attention completely.

I abandoned my post under the far end of the ship, swimming deeper than I had been, hoping to avoid harpoons, cannon fire, and, seas-forbid, nets. I reached the other side of the ship just to see another body plunge into the water.

I launched myself up, feeling the pull toward it. They wore the white of the hunter. Surely my feeling of rightness, of peace, came from the kill I was going to make. I would claim another life that was owed to me, another life that had helped take mine.

I reached the body, but I froze when I looked closer.

It was a woman.

Impossible. The hunters were all men.

The sirens weren't supposed to hurt women, but we did hurt hunters.

I couldn't decide what to do. I pulled closer to her, wanting to get a better look.

I ignored the metal poking out of her. That wasn't of interest to me unless I decided to save her. Right now, I needed to see her face.

The surface-dweller's short blond hair was ringing their head like a halo, and her eyes were closed, but there was something familiar about her face. The feeling was wiggling around in the back of my mind, making me uncomfortable. I quickly shoved it away. It wasn't important. Whoever this was, they couldn't mean anything to me.

They were a hunter, and I was about to make them my prey.

# Chapter Thirty Three
## Ray

A hazy calm swept over me as I cracked open my eyes. I was cold but felt weightless. I could barely feel my body around me and was blessedly detached from the pain I knew I would have been feeling if I were still alive.

When I noticed the angel floating in front of me with her perfect dark curls and icy blue eyes, I knew I was in the Realm of the Gods.

"Cor–" was all I managed before the world went dark again.

# CHAPTER THIRTY FOUR
## Coral

She called me 'Cor', I thought, freezing. When the surface-dweller had opened her eyes, she had called me 'Cor'. Was it possible she knew me from before?

'Cor' was all I could remember of my old life, of my old name when the others took me in. Charia and the others decided to call me 'Coral' like the reefs. I liked it well enough, but no one should have known that except my sisters, but this hunter knew.

I held the huntress at arm's length as I watched her, trying to decide what to do with her. She couldn't have known me. I didn't know what sort of power the hunters had, but I couldn't trust her. The lack of trust didn't change the feeling of rightness, of peace, when I looked at her, though.

The siren instincts in me were just as confused.

Normally the siren overruled what I wanted in situations like this, but I found my siren and I were just as conflicted. As a hunter, this woman deserved death, but as the moments passed, I felt the feeling of peace starting to dissolve into panic. Whoever the surface-dweller was, whatever they were, it was clear that the seas had led me to her, and it likely wasn't just to watch her die.

*You better not make me regret this*, I thought to her just in case she could somehow hear me, before I pressed my lips to hers, breathing life back into her in a nick of time.

I pulled the piece of metal out of her and brushed my fingers over the wound, watching as her skin slowly knit itself back together. I needed to get her to the surface safely and quickly.

Without thinking hard about it, I carried us toward the pirates' ship. Charia always said they were our allies, and they would help me help her.

I swam faster, closing the distance, when I heard gasps behind me. The surface-dweller was running out of air. I pushed myself faster and breached the surface at the last possible moment, hoping we were out of range of the hunters, but I wasn't entirely sure. It would've been safer to stay below, but I couldn't let the little huntress die after just having saved her life.

I stayed underneath her, holding her steady on the water. I told myself I was using her as a shield, and it certainly wasn't compassion, but I couldn't even fool myself.

I heard a commotion coming from the pirates' ship and hoped that meant they saw her. I needed to get out of the open.

I swam her a little closer, and they threw down a rope. I let go of her, waiting for her to grab it, but she started to sink below the water again. I shook her, but she didn't move.

I pulled her under again, planting another kiss on her lips, hoping it would wake her, but still nothing.

I was too focused on her to notice the harpoon rushing toward me. Her eyes cracked open, and she cracked a small smile before her eyes widened in horror and she gripped my arm, moving me a little closer to her. It wasn't far, but it was enough, since the harpoon tore through my side instead of skewering me.

The move seemed to have zapped all her strength though, since her eyes closed again.

The pain was lancing through me. I needed my sisters and we needed to get out of here before anyone else got hurt. I was pulling her to the surface when a net crashed around us. I lost my grip on her as the net closed around us. Her body banged into mine as I fought uselessly to free us.

I struggled against the ropes, but it was no use. I felt the net being pulled up and felt the hopelessness wash over me. I reached for my seaweed bracelet, considering. I had a moment or two to decide. I was considering ingesting the poison when I noticed the net was being pulled up toward the pirates' ship, not the hunters.

I dropped my wrist and was forced to hold the huntress against me as we were propelled into the air. The bracelet came loose. I grabbed for it but was too late and had to watch in despair as it fell from the net to the water below. I felt my shock move to anger as I saw the pirates lugging us up. They were supposed to be our allies, and yet they had captured me.

They yanked us up and up until they finally hoisted us onboard. The huntress's body slamming on top of mine when the net crashed onto the deck.

There was yelling, so much yelling, that stopped when a tall curly haired girl with a comically large hat pushed through the rest.

"There's a siren!" she yelled.

Another girl rushed in behind her, and I gasped. She was human, unmistakably on two legs, and yet she had the eyes of a sister and I felt drawn to her, like my heart knew her the same way I felt with my sisters.

"Cut them out!" Funny Hat yelled, and someone quickly did. Then, they grabbed the huntress from me, and Funny Hat pointed in my direction, talking to the land siren. "We have to throw her back!"

I was starting to like her. Maybe we were allies after all. "We can't!" the land siren argued. My eyes narrowed. Apparently, my feelings weren't to be trusted. First, I was foolish enough to save a hunter, and now I was trapped on a pirate ship. "She's hurt," she continued, moving to me, "Seas, I'm so sorry, sister, but we can't send you into open water like that."

I blinked, looking down at my side, only now noticing the blue blood oozing out of it.

Funny Hat nodded. "You're right." She then turned to me and said, "We'll have you fixed up in no time, Captain's honor." Her eyes fell on the crowd and, pointing at a scowling girl with a dark braid, she said, "Neta, go get Flora." The girl ran off, but Funny Hat didn't stop there. She pointed at another. This one had hair the color of a sunset. "Addie, go draw a bath. We want our guest to feel welcome."

Funny Hat and the land siren advanced on me, so I showed them my teeth, snarling at them. Allies or not, I didn't know them, and I was injured and out of the water. I didn't want them near me.

The land siren moved in front of Funny Hat and said calmly, "I know this isn't what you want, but it's what you need. We're going to help you, but we can only do that if we can get you off the deck and into a bath. We can't let you into the water. The hunters would kill you before your sisters could heal you, so we'll give you water to rest in until your wounds are healed. Then I swear by the seas and Nema herself, we'll let you go. Do you understand?" she asked.

I wasn't sure if I could trust them, but flipping my fins on land wouldn't get me too far, so I just nodded and let them use the net to pull me up and suspend me between them.

She and Funny Hat brought me what they called a bath, which turned out to be a container of water barely large enough for my entire body to be submerged.

They dipped me into it, gently letting the net down with me. The water felt soothing on my skin and scales. They hadn't been dry for long, but it had been long enough to itch. The pain in my side dulled too with the cooling embrace of the water. All at once, I realized how tired I was from the battle. I could barely keep my head above water, but that was more than fine with me. With a nod of thanks at Funny Hat and the land siren, I let myself sink beneath the surface and closed my eyes, giving in to the soothing lull and letting myself drift off to sleep.

# Chapter Thirty Five

## Ray

I groaned, turning over as pain and panic radiated through my body. The last thing I remembered was being stabbed by Captain Butcher.

Fear shot through me. If I wasn't dead–and the pain lancing through me assured me I wasn't–then I was worse than dead. I was a prisoner of the Saints, of the butcher of the seas, and I very much doubted they would bring me back to the Convent in one piece.

I tried to settle my breathing as much as I could and parse out my surroundings. If I was still alive, they must still want something from me. I moved incrementally, trying to test my range of motion to see if I was restrained. I didn't want to move too much in case someone was watching me. The longer they thought I was out, the better. I needed to learn everything I could about where I was if I had any hope of survival.

"I know you're awake," a deadpan voice said from a few feet away.

I groaned and fully opened my eyes, blinking against the light. I sat up as quickly as I dared. I was in what looked like a storage room, not a holding cell, and I surprisingly wasn't restrained. Although with the pain I was in I doubt I could put up much of a fight, so it made sense they didn't bother. What didn't make sense was the ship's sail they had me wrapped in. I was grateful for the blanket, of course, but I couldn't understand the kindness.

I looked down and was grateful I couldn't see any blood. I would have to check my injuries soon, but that could wait.

Since I didn't appear to be in immediate danger of dying where I lay, I turned to the voice and then scrambled back in alarm. My gasp turned into a groan when I hit the wall at my back, hard.

There was a large bathing tub in the chamber with me, and I could see the tips of a scaled tail jutting out.

I was stuck in here with a seas damned siren.

Either I was marked for death with the siren, or they hoped she would finish the job for them. Either way, this wasn't looking good.

I pulled myself up slowly, surprised to find I was more sore than in pain. My head hurt, but the rest of my body didn't seem to understand it had just been stabbed, but I wasn't complaining. I made my way to the door, careful not to turn my back on the tub. When I felt the door to my back, I fumbled around for the handle.

"What are you doing?" came the voice again, a musical lilt of curiosity shining through.

"Looking for a way out of here."

"Wouldn't be a very good holding cell if the door were unlocked."

"Wouldn't be a very good pirate if I didn't try," I shot back as my hand found the handle. Of course, it was locked.

"Since you're not a pirate, it hardly matters if you're a good one."

I jiggled the handle a few more times, testing it, but it was locked.

"Can I trust you not to try anything if I turn around?"

"Can *you* trust *me*? Unlikely."

I sighed, taking a breath before turning my back on her, anyway. I figured there wasn't much she could do to me from the tub, and I was hoping to make it out of there before finding out I was wrong.

I appraised the lock and was happy to find it was similar to the ones on our ship. I reached for my dagger with a smile before remembering my blade was lost. The last place I had seen it was embedded in my gut as

I plummeted to the seas, but that couldn't have been right. Maybe I had been stabbed, but I certainly hadn't fallen if I were here now, being held captive. They wouldn't have cared enough to fish me out of the water when I was as good as dead.

I turned back to the tub with a frustrated huff. "Aren't you going to say anything?"

"Our captors will probably be back soon," the tub replied.

"Do they know I'm awake?"

"If they did, they would be here. They were quite anxious to see you."

I shivered at that. The last thing I wanted was for the Saints to get their hands back on me. "If I go back to my corner and pretend to be asleep when they come in, will you tell them I'm pretending?"

There was silence before she said, "Probably."

Her top half was out of the water now, but she was facing the wall. She wouldn't even look at me. I should probably be grateful. I had never been this close to a siren before, and perhaps I should have been more concerned, but curiosity was pulling at me. I wanted to know what she looked like up close.

I hoped my life wouldn't end on this ship, but even if it didn't and I lived a long, happy life, I didn't think I would ever have this opportunity again to be this close to a siren.

Of course, 'close' was relative since I was about as far as I could be from her in our enclosed space.

I looked back at the corner I had woken up in with the sail-turned-blanket and thought about going to curl up there, anyway. I felt drained enough that I might actually fall back asleep, but I knew it was futile since she planned to tell our captors I had recovered enough to move. I couldn't help wondering why she would, though, and before I could think better of it, the question was out of my mouth.

Frustration and helplessness seeped into my voice. "Why would you help them?"

"I might not like them much right now, but I dislike you more."

Her tone left no doubt it was true, but I couldn't even begin to understand her meaning.

"Why? What could I have possibly done to make you hate me more than the heretics?"

She spun around, and the sight of her knocked me to my knees. I couldn't believe I hadn't recognized her from the back. Her dark hair was exactly the same, and her shoulders were the same ones I trailed kisses down. Now that she had turned, I could see her face was largely the same, too. She was paler now, which made sense since she wasn't in the sun as much.

I had never seen her face so distorted by anger, but it was unmistakably hers. Her blue eyes were slightly distorted, slightly unnatural with the swirling movement of the siren magic, but they were still hers.

I almost didn't hear her words through the million thoughts that all fought for dominance.

"Cora," rushed past my lips.

At the same time, she said bitterly, "You're the reason I'm here."

Tears were running down my face, as I took her in fully. Where her legs used to be, she had a violet purple tail that glistened as she flicked it in the water. The scales of her tail traveled up past her waist, turning from purple to blue and splitting in two, looking almost like a corset the way they covered her chest.

I had never been close enough to the sirens to realize they didn't wear tops. They didn't need to since the scales covered them.

Siren or not, there was no mistaking it was her.

She was watching me through those blue sea eyes that were so familiar to me. The distrust and anger in them was unfamiliar, and so was the swirling, cloudy motion of them, but they were her eyes. She was a siren and she was angry, but it was a seas blessed miracle that she was even here. My Cora was still alive.

I sprang to my feet and closed the distance between us. I got my arms wrapped around her for a brief moment before she pushed me away. Then her hand was in my hair and she pushed my face into the water.

I inhaled water in my shock and tried to fight her grip, but I couldn't pry her hands off of me, and I couldn't make sense of what was happening.

Cora was *here*.

Cora was *alive*.

Cora was a *siren*.

Cora was trying to *kill* me.

I loved her deeply, but not enough to make it easy for her. She would have to try harder than that to get rid of me.

I braced my legs on the outside of the tub and pushed as hard as I could.

I felt the searing pain of hair pulling from my scalp as I sprung from her grip and away from her. The lungful of air I pulled in made the pain feel worth it.

"What's wrong with you?" I gasped out.

The door opened behind us and I flung myself back toward the corner I woke up in, wanting to be father from Cora the siren, and farther from the door.

I grabbed the sail and wrapped it around myself, trying to dry off a little.

"Ray! You're awake!"

I whipped around to see Scyla beaming at me from across the room.

"You came to rescue me?" I asked quickly, in a much quieter tone. The last thing I wanted was to alert my captors to the rescue party.

She furrowed her brows, looking at me closer, "Are you okay?"

I felt the back of my head, checking for blood. Thankfully, my hand came away without any. My head was tender, but I was fine.

"I am now," I grinned. She took a step towards me, only to be yanked back.

Tess had pulled her back and then stepped in front of her. "You know the rules," she said, leveling a stare at Scyla that I shrunk back from. Tess turned back to me and said, not unkindly, "You're safe. We got you back to the ship by no small miracle, thank the goddess. How are you feeling?"

I knew she was angry, but was Tess really that determined to punish me that they were keeping me in here?

I considered a moment, "Well, I have a killer headache, and a broken heart since my girlfriend is a siren and just tried to murder me, but since I think I was stabbed earlier today, I'd say I'm doing well."

Scyla and Tess exchanged a look, but surprisingly, neither said anything.

I nodded, turning to her tub. I said slowly, "She's angry at me and said it was my fault she was here." I turned back to the tub, but Cora was watching Tess instead of me. I still addressed her when I added, "And you're not wrong. I'm so sorry. It was all my fault."

Scyla took another step toward me, but Tess yanked her back. She grunted in frustration, spinning back to face her. "Come on, she's clearly still Ray, and she needs a hug."

It occurred to me then that neither of them had gotten any closer to me than they had to Cora. They were treating both of us with caution. "If this is our ship, why am I in here?" I asked carefully.

"It's a safety precaution," Tess said carefully.

"We figured you could use the rest," Scyla added. "Goddess knows the rest of us don't shut up long enough for anyone to get any shut-eye around here."

I gave her my best smile, but I knew it probably looked as pitiful as I was feeling.

"It's not for long. We'll explain after you get a bit more sleep," Scyla assured me.

The last thing on my mind right now was sleep. There was no way I was going to be able to fall asleep with all the adrenaline coursing through my veins.

Tess must've read my mind since she said, "Don't worry, we brought you something for that and the nasty headache I'm sure you have from the other healing draughts."

That explained it.

I expected her to hand me something, but instead, she rolled it to me. The door creaked open again, and Addie came in with a sad smile and an overflowing tray of food.

"I'm so glad you're okay," she said. She took a step toward me but glanced at Tess before getting any closer. Tess shook her head, and Addie set the tray down on the floor in front of her across the room before leaving with one more apologetic glance at me.

I looked over the items, wondering what sirens liked. I was sure she was used to fish and seaweed, but I wondered if she would eat human food now that she was above the water.

"What about me?" Cora asked.

I looked over at her in surprise. Yes, she had just tried to drown me, but I hadn't thought for a moment about not feeding her. I was going to be more careful, of course, but I wasn't going to starve her.

Tess looked at her skeptically. "Can I get close to you without you trying to hurt me?"

Cora shrugged, "Are you brave enough to find out, pirate?"

"Cora wouldn't hurt anyone," I said quickly.

She finally turned to look at me again. "My name is Coral, and I most certainly do hurt people, but you're right, my sisters have a pact with the pirates. They're safe with me. You," she said, grinning at me, showing unnaturally pointed teeth that made me gulp, "are another story."

Tess and Scyla exchanged concerned looks, but I waved it off. "It's fine. Cora—I mean, Coral—and I are just getting reacquainted." They didn't look reassured, so I added, "I promise she won't hurt me."

"You don't speak for me," she bit out.

Tess looked between Coral and me before looking back at Scyla and saying, "We really don't have much of a choice but to trust them."

She looked at Coral and said, "I'm claiming Ray. If anything happens to her by your hand, consider the truce broken."

Coral looked like she was going to say something, but then turned away with a huff, saying, "Worthless surface-dwellers," under her breath.

Tess turned her attention back to me. "Have something to eat and take the draught. We'll come back and explain everything after you get some more sleep. Your body needs more rest to heal."

Tess ushered Scyla out of the room. Once they closed the door, I pulled myself to my feet and crossed the room. "Do you want anything?" I asked in the direction of Coral's tub.

"From you? I'd rather starve."

It killed me to hear how much she hated me, but it made sense that becoming a siren had changed her. I needed to get to know the new her. I had won her over once, and I hoped I could do it again.

I grabbed an orange off the tray before sliding the rest over to her. It came to a stop right before the tub, but it was well within her reach. I moved back to my corner and peeled the orange, chewing it slowly. I was struggling to believe this wasn't a dream. Being locked in storage on my own ship with my siren girlfriend who hated me sounded more like a nightmare than real life.

I picked up the draught and drained it, knowing the crew would have my head if I didn't. They had become my family, and they were fiercely protective. I put the last piece of orange peel down and grabbed the sail blanket, and then the world went dark.

# Chapter Thirty Six
## Coral

I watched the little huntress fall asleep, waiting until she had been out for a good few minutes before moving. I swished my tail, splashing in her direction, but there was no response.

Perfect.

I leaned over and surveyed the tray, grabbing the first thing that smelled good, grateful she wasn't awake to see. The only thing I hated more than being offered help was needing it, and unfortunately, thanks to her, I was a fish out of water.

I was at her mercy and, even worse, I was still wounded. The hunters had hit me because of the huntress, and because I didn't let go of her, I was dragged away from the sea and my sisters who could have healed me. Worse still, I had sapped my own strength healing her, an act I still didn't understand and regretted with every waking moment. Now I was far weaker than I would have been. I couldn't have healed myself since we couldn't heal our own bodies, but if I had left her for dead, I would be safely with my sisters now instead of above my home, floating around on a pirate ship.

I should have let her die. Clearly, it's what she would have done to me. She had attacked me to finish the job almost the first moment she got. She had her arms wrapped around me before I could react.

Maybe trying to drown her was a bit of an overreaction, but she was attacking me—until the other surface-dwellers came in, anyway.

She was dangerous the way she spun the story to make me the villain. She told them I attacked her. She even called me her girlfriend. The lies were laughable, and I still couldn't believe the pirates had believed it and taken her side.

When I made it back to my sisters, I was going to have to talk to Charia about our truce with the pirates. They had sided with a hunter over me and were keeping me a prisoner here. That was hardly friendly behavior.

I started feeling sleepy after having only eaten a little bit. I let myself slide under the water and drift off to sleep.

# Chapter Thirty Seven
## Coral

When I woke sometime later, the water around me had cooled, losing the warmth it had first held. I welcomed the change, the cooler waters reminding me more of the sea. The sea was the only home I had known, and I hated being separated from it, all thanks to that seas damned huntress and my stupid moment of weakness.

I welcomed the cool water brushing against my tail, the water reflecting the purple of my scales as the light danced over me.

As far as cages go, I supposed it could have been far worse. It also could have been far better if it weren't for my present company. She was a near-constant reminder of how reckless and stupid I had been. I should have let her drown.

She was still sleeping, and I welcomed the silence, a reprieve from her attention.

Even sleep couldn't hide the monster she was, but at least in her sleep I could study her without being observed myself.

Her features were softer than they should be for the monster that she was. Her yellowy hair fell just above her shoulders and her face had a dusting of freckles. I hated that I liked them. In sleep, she looked deceptively harmless, and her features weren't unpleasant to look at.

There was a knock at the door that had me turning to glare, my siren instincts perking up for the first time in days. Where was my siren when

I needed her, when I wanted to tear out the little huntress's throat? But better late than never, I supposed.

I was sure it was Funny Hat, the land siren, and their friends back to check on us again. I wasn't sure if I trusted them, though. My sisters and I had believed these humans to be harmless.

I had yet to decide if we were wrong.

They often fought alongside us to free those in need and to help us escape the hunters, but they seemed inexplicably fond of this huntress.

They hadn't harmed me, but they also hadn't released me and were keeping me here with her. Those were slights I wouldn't be quick to forgive.

Not for the first time, I wondered if I was guarding the huntress or if she was guarding me.

I knew that if my sisters believed me to be in danger, they would have come for me. The fact that the ship hadn't been attacked proved that they trusted the pirates. For better or worse, this ship and its humans were our allies. I just hoped Charia's faith in them wasn't misplaced.

The door creaked, and I glanced over at the huntress, seeing her slowly wake. Eyeing her warily, I called out to the entering human as loudly as I dared, "Careful, she's awake."

The stirring huntress shot me an indignant look as the remains of sleep faded from her seaweed-colored eyes. "It's not me they need to be worried about."

I huffed out a laugh. "Powerful or not, I'm contained. I can't say the same for you."

The door opened the rest of the way and Funny Hat came in asking, "How are you both feeling?"

At the same time, the huntress and I began, "I'm fine, but she's—"

We looked at each other, startled.

She cocked an eyebrow at me and finished, "Difficult."

"Dangerous," I bit out, finishing my sentence. Her face didn't fall, though. It seemed that along with regaining her strength, she also regained her nerve. I begrudgingly respected her a bit more for it.

It had been grating, watching her flinch at my words, like she had feelings that could be hurt. The idea of a hunter with feelings was laughable. They considered us the monsters, but they were the ones hunting us.

The huntress turned back to the woman and asked, "Have I passed the test?"

Funny Hat looked wary, but said, "You seem normal enough. Love, do you mind?"

"Not at all," the land siren said, stepping into the room. I should have been used to her by now, but her voice still had an effect on me. It was instantly soothing, like waves lapping at my tail.

She walked over to the huntress, getting within arm's reach. "Be careful!" I warned.

"It's alright, don't worry about me."

But I was worried. The huntress had attacked me, and my heart knew this land siren was of the sea, like I was. If I felt that, surely the huntress would, too, and would try to hurt her.

The huntress didn't make a move toward her, and for once, I was happy to be proven wrong.

The land siren moved the huntress's face back and forth, looking into her eyes, and then called back to Funny Hat, "I don't understand how, but she's fine for now."

"Perfect," Funny Hat said, grinning. "Just in time."

"Time for what?" I asked, not liking the sound of it or the fact that Funny Hat and the land siren didn't seem appropriately concerned about the huntress.

"Time to give you two a breather from each other," Funny Hat said. "Besides, Mel wants to talk to you," Funny Hat said, looking at me.

She looked at the land siren, Mel apparently, and said, "I'll take Ray, and you can talk to—" She paused and looked at me.

"Coral," I said.

It made sense they were taking the huntress for questioning, and I was anxious to talk to the land siren to find out more about her.

She didn't make any sense. She had the eyes of my sisters, a mirror to my own with the swirling depths of the ocean in them. It wasn't possible for many reasons, but most importantly, because she was standing there. Standing. On legs.

Funny Hat clapped a hand on the huntress's back. "Come on, let's give them some space." She guided the huntress to the door. Before Funny Hat closed it behind herself, she gave the land siren, Mel, a look and said, "Go easy on our guest."

Mel rolled her eyes and said, "You worry too much, love. She'll be fine."

To my surprise, the huntress looked over her shoulder at me once more, too. I saw her concern and did my best to ignore it. She must have been concerned for herself. After all, she was the one being taken away for questioning. Finally. It was about time they treated her like the enemy she was.

With that, Funny Hat shut the door behind herself and the huntress. I finally relaxed a little with them out of sight.

The land siren moved closer to me, sitting a few feet away from my tub. She was within reach, making it clear that she either didn't consider me a threat, or she trusted me.

"Mel," I said, testing her name on my tongue to break the silence.

"It's short for Melody," she said with a shy smile. "You might've heard the name before. Does Charia still talk about me?"

I bolted straight up at that. "You know Charia?"

She nodded, grinning. "She and I used to be the best of friends. I know she doesn't understand my choices, but I hope she thinks about me every once in a while. I think about her a lot, too."

"Wait, were you—are you—" I began, not knowing how to ask, before settling for, "But you have legs?"

"Usually. I was a siren for a long time, and now I don't really know what I am. I was captured by the White Robes—"

"Who are the White Robes?"

"Oh yes, sorry, the hunters. The pirates call them the White Robes. They call themselves the Saints."

"Why do surface-dwellers insist on having five million names for everything?"

She laughed at that. "It's true, and as long as I've been with them, I couldn't tell you why. Maybe it makes them feel in control to put a name to things. It's hard to know."

"So, the hunters captured you?"

She nodded gravely. "They did. They held me there as siren repellant," she spat out. "They did unspeakable things to me until I wished I was dead, but Charia didn't come for me. I knew they were worried about getting me killed in the rescue, but that would've been preferable to what they did to me."

No wonder Charia made us all wear the poison seaweed. She had lost Melody to the hunters, and wasn't willing to lose another.

"They were thrilled when they discovered I could assume the anatomy of a surface-dweller."

I had been trying to let her tell her story, but I had to interrupt. "Does that mean you can grow legs whenever you want them? Could you have a tail now if you wanted?"

She grinned. "If I hopped in the tub with you, yes."

"What? How?"

"I don't think all of our sisters know. I wouldn't have found it out on my own either, but when the hunters kept me dry for too long, my scales felt itchy for a few minutes before disappearing entirely, and my tail separated into two legs. The first time it happened, I thought I was dying. The hunters ran a lot of cruel tests on me, but it gave me the knowledge I have now. If I fully submerge myself in water and breathe it in, I can trigger the transformation again."

"Does that mean–could I–" I stopped, not sure I wanted to know.

She gave me an apologetic smile. "I'm not sure. As far as I know, I'm the only one to have done it. You would have to try it out on your own to learn the truth, but yes, I do think you could. I doubt it's unique to me."

"So, what happened after the hunters? Why are you up here with the pirates instead of under the seas with Charia and the rest of the pod?"

A far-off look came over her face. "The pirates–well, Tess mainly–rescued me from the hunters. She didn't know I was there, but when she found me, she didn't hesitate to try to get me to safety, at a large risk to herself. I was incredibly grateful to her. It was more than my sisters had done for me. I know they were trying to protect me and keep me alive by not attacking, but I was very angry back then. When they freed me, I decided to stay with them for a little while. It was the first decision I had made for myself in... I don't know how long. I figured I would sail with them for a while and let my anger cool before rejoining Charia and the rest of our sisters. By the time my anger was a distant memory, my heart was elsewhere."

"You fell in love with being a pirate?" I asked skeptically.

She laughed at that. "I fell in love with a pirate. The pirating is a fun bonus."

"Funny Hat?" I asked before I thought to try to recall her name.

Melody barked out a laugh. "Assuming you're talking about Tess, our Captain, then yes. I can't wait to tell her you said that. I've been telling her for ages that the hat is ridiculous."

"So, if you're a siren and our pods are friends to the pirates, why am I still here?" I asked bluntly.

The smile immediately dropped from her face. "The hunters haven't gone far. They haven't attacked again since our fight a couple of days ago, but they're sticking close. They're ruthless, and I don't trust them not to cut you down the moment you jump ship."

"They're no match for me."

She chuckled. "In top condition, I'm sure that's true, but you're hurt."

I twisted away from her, instinctually hiding my side. It was healing, but she was right. There was still pain.

"And they don't play fair anymore. Their experiments on me gave them more tricks than they had any right knowing. The smart ones plug their ears, so our songs don't work."

That explained why some of our attacks weren't as successful as they should have been and why Charia said their attacks were a lot more deadly to us than they used to be.

"So, how long do you plan to keep me here?"

"We're hoping to get away from them in another day or two, but I'm hoping you might stay a little longer to help us with Ray. We're worried."

The huntress. I could understand why they would be concerned about the safety of having her on board, but I didn't understand what they planned to do with her. "You want me to keep watch over her?"

Melody's shoulders slumped in relief. "Exactly. We're worried about her possibly undergoing the transition. I'm assuming you used your power on her to help her, right?"

I had, and I was still regretting it. I hadn't even stopped to think about the implications. Normally, the transition was quick, but we were usually in the water. "You think she might turn into a siren?" I asked, worrying about the answer.

A siren that sided with the hunters. If they didn't kill her on sight, she would be a plague on the seas. She could hunt us for them. There would be no escaping her. *What had I done?*

"She hasn't yet, and she seems normal, but until we can be sure, she has to stay isolated. You know how difficult it is to think past the instincts when you first turn. We can't have her loose on the ship if that happens."

It made sense. Even now, I still struggled to think past the siren instincts. "I made a mess of things saving her," I said quietly.

She quickly shook her head. "Not at all. I don't know why you chose to save her, but we're grateful all the same. I don't think she will turn, but if she does, having you here would help. If she doesn't remember any of us, she might still listen to you."

"Why in the seas would she listen to me?"

"Because you turned her. She'll feel a connection with you."

I considered that and had to admit it made sense. I felt a strong connection with Charia. She had saved me and granted me a new life.

I understood that, but what I couldn't understand was why they cared about the huntress at all. The pirates hadn't shied away from killing hunters in the past. I wondered if maybe it was because this hunter was a woman. Maybe my little huntress had them wrapped around her finger. I froze at the thought. I wasn't sure when I had started thinking of her as *my* huntress. She wasn't mine, although maybe she was, now that I agreed to the pirates' request to keep an eye on her.

I only had two choices: I could either leave the first chance I got, worrying for all time that I had let loose a monster loyal to the hunters, or I could stay and do my best to fix the mess I created.

I had chosen to save her and we were here with the pirates for the time being anyway. I couldn't undo any of that, but what I could do was learn more from Melody about the pirates and myself. If I had to keep an eye on my little huntress to do that, I supposed I could.

"I'll do it if you swear on the seas that if she turns, you'll put her down."

Her eyes widened in alarm. "There has to be another way. If she turns, she can be controlled. She'll listen to you."

I sighed, considering. If she did listen to me, then Melody was right, and she wouldn't be a threat. "Okay," I amended, "if she isn't able to be controlled or to control it, she doesn't live to be a monster."

Melody closed her eyes for a moment and whispered, "Seas help us if that's the case. Tess will kill me, but yes, if she's truly a threat, she'll be dealt with."

"Swear it on the seas."

"I swear on the seas that if Ray becomes an uncontrollable monster, we'll end her life. It's what she would want anyway, but it won't come to that. She's strong-willed. If she does transform, she'll be able to handle it."

Her strong will was exactly what I *was* worried about. If she remembered herself well enough, she could be the deadliest weapon in the hunters' arsenal. But Melody had sworn. Once a siren, always a siren. She wouldn't make the oath without knowing she could and would follow through.

"And swear on the seas that when we're clear of the hunters and this problem is... solved, I'll be free to rejoin my sisters."

Melody nodded quickly. "I swear it. Tess doesn't keep unwilling guests on the ship. If you weren't injured, I would have offered you the choice now. Speaking of which, our healer is making a salve for your wound. It won't help as much as a sister could have, but it should still help. I would offer to help myself, but I haven't transformed in so long that the gift doesn't work for me anymore."

"Why haven't you transformed?" I asked.

Even if I was able to have legs, I couldn't imagine ever being willing to give up my tail like she had.

"I have too much to lose in this new life of mine. I'm worried that if I transform, the instincts would take over again, and I wouldn't be myself."

I understood the fear. They were generally almost impossible to fight. There was something about being on the ship that was giving me peace from them for a little while, and while I still would much rather be underwater, I could understand the appeal of not having to fight a part of herself to think clearly.

"Thank you for helping us," she said with another smile. "Tess'll bring Ray back shortly, and I promise we won't keep either of you in here much longer. In a couple more days, if she hasn't turned, we'll know she's safe."

I watched her leave, digesting what I had learned. I couldn't believe there was a chance that sirens were able to come on land freely. I wondered if Melody was the first person to do it, or if there were others out there like us who chose to live among the surface dwellers.

The sea was my home, and I would never give that up, but I was sure there were advantages to having legs. Maybe it would be worth trying.

# CHAPTER THIRTY EIGHT
# Ray

When Tess shut the door to the storage room on Mel and Coral, she pulled me into a fierce hug.

"Thank the goddess and the seas you're alright!" she said, patting me on the back before letting me go. There was a goofy grin on her face that had me grinning back.

"Glad to be back, Captain."

"Come on, let's go to my office before the rest of the crew sees you. I wasn't supposed to touch you, and Mel's going to be even more pissed if the rest of the crew tackles you."

I laughed at that and followed her.

I was confused by the quiet until I checked the portholes and saw it was the middle of the night. For our ship, though, it was still an unusually quiet night.

"We're not out of the woods yet with the hunters. Everyone's been on high alert, grabbing sleep when they can."

She pulled open the door to her office and shoved me in. When she shut it behind her, she leaned back and huffed out a breath. "You're so lucky I'm too relieved you're alive to kill you myself. That stunt you pulled was reckless and dangerous."

It was hard to believe that it had only been a few days ago that I was willing to get myself killed to avenge Cora, who apparently was now Coral the siren. "I know, I'm so sorry."

"If you ever do something that stupid without warning me first, your ass is being dropped at the next port. I won't be lied to, and I won't be ignored. I expect you to listen to me, but I don't expect to be obeyed without question. If I had thought for even a second that you would try to pull off a solo mission like that, we would've figured something else out, okay?"

"Really?"

"Really. I mean it when I say we're family. I may be the one in charge, but everyone's voice matters." She sighed before adding, "And I let you down. I'm sorry I didn't listen to you when you came to me. I knew it was a reckless plan, but I should have talked to you more about it. I should have listened to you. I'm sorry you felt like you had to do that on your own."

"I'm sorry too. I never meant to put Scyla in danger."

"That's Scyla's battle to fight with you. She chose to go. That has nothing to do with me. What you should be apologizing for was endangering the life of my newest recruit."

I blinked, quiet for a moment, wondering if maybe my head was in worse shape than I thought. "I promise only Scyla and I went on the mission."

She nodded, "Yes, and I'm angry with you for endangering your own life. I happen to value it even if you don't, and I know everyone here feels the same. I'll be damned if you go careening off into another suicide mission without knowing that I'd bring you back from a watery grave to kill you myself if you pull another stunt like that."

The tears started to well up in my eyes. I blinked fiercely, but a couple fell. "I thought it would be worth it. They hurt Cora. She was gone because of them. Now she's back, but she's changed and I don't know what to think."

Tess's face fell, and she sighed. "I knew I should've had Addie here. Emotions aren't my specialty, but bring it in, kid." She opened her arms to me, and I let her hug me again.

I hugged her long enough to regain my composure. When I pulled back, she pulled out a chair, saying, "Take a seat. You're gonna need one for what I've got to tell you."

I sat quickly. She'd been doing this for years. She had to have some idea of what was going on. "Do you know what's happened to her? She might just be pissed at me that she was claimed by the sea. She told me it was my fault she was here. I didn't think she would blame me, at least, she wouldn't have before, but–"

"No, no," she cut me off. "There's a lot I need to tell you about the transformation. Mel's told me everything she knows, which, lucky for us, is a whole lot. She was underwater for far longer than she has been on land. I haven't told the rest of the crew this, though, only Neta.  I thought it was too cruel, but now with your Cora on board, we'll have to break it to them."

"Break what to them?"

She sighed and said slowly, "There's something about the transformation that changes a person."

I looked at her pointedly.

She cracked a grin. "Besides the tail and scales, obviously. The transformation makes them more animal-like, more driven by instinct, and in their case, the instincts of the siren."

"Which are?"

"To protect those they love, to protect the vulnerable, and to neutralize any threats to those they protect."

"That doesn't sound too bad," I said slowly, "but that doesn't explain how she's been acting, or why she tried to drown me."

She straightened up, alarm painting her features. "She tried to drown you in the seas?"

"No, in her tub. When she showed me her face, even with the tail and her changed eyes, I knew it was her. I ran to her and tried to hug her and got a face full of water instead."

Tess considered before saying, "Maybe she thought you were attacking her?"

"I would never!"

"Of course I know that, but maybe she doesn't. Still, it makes no sense. I don't know why she would try to drown you after saving you."

"She saved me?"

"She pulled you out of the water and dragged you to our ship. She got hit with a harpoon while protecting you, and then she got caught in our net. We didn't realize it in the chaos until she was already on deck and by then it was sheer chaos in the water. We couldn't let her go in her injured state."

"She saved me?" I repeated, trying to remember the battle. When I thought hard, I did remember a flash of purple scales and dark hair floating in front of me. I remembered calling out, "Cor." Then there was nothing until I woke up in the storage room.

"She did, but she's not herself after the transformation. Sirens don't remember their old human lives. Mel thinks it's the Goddess's way of easing the difficult transition."

She didn't remember me. Coralina, the light in the darkness of my life, didn't remember me. I had found her just to lose her all over again.

"Is there anything I can do? Will she ever remember me?"

Tess's eyes reflected my pain. "We're not sure. Mel thinks it's worth it to try and jog her memory. We're going to keep you in there with her. Maybe it'll help her to remember if she talks to you more. Just–" She stopped and inhaled before continuing, "Just swear you'll be careful. We don't know how dangerous she is, and I don't want her to hurt you."

"She wouldn't. She saved me."

"And then apparently tried to drown you."

"Not hard, though. If she wanted me dead, I would be."

"Fair enough, but still, swear on your honor as a Daughter that you'll be careful."

"I swear it. Wouldn't want to give you a heart attack. I figure you probably need at least another week to recover until I pull something else that reckless."

She shook her head in disapproval, undermined by her badly hidden grin, "I don't know whether to laugh or cry. I can see Scyla's been a terrible influence on you already."

"I was already terrible," I said, grinning.

"Spoken like a true-blue Daughter of the Deep." She stood up, grabbing a small green glass jar from her desk and pocketing it before gesturing to the door. "Come on, I should probably get you back. Mel is a little paranoid that you could be undergoing a slow transformation from the magic Cora used to heal you and would kill me if I kept you away much longer."

"What?!" I exclaimed. "Is that possible?"

"Highly unlikely. If you were going to turn, I'm sure you would've done it already, but Mel is insisting we wait a few more days before letting you back out with the rest of us rabble, just to be sure."

She opened the door and was already through it. I hopped up, rushing after her.

"You just dropped the news that I might be turning into a siren and expect me to be calm about it?"

"It's been three days. If you were going to turn, I'm sure it would've happened already. Mel's worried over nothing, but it wouldn't hurt to have you and Cora forced into a small space together. It might help trigger her memory."

"What if I turn, though? I could hurt someone!"

"If you do turn, you won't hurt Cora. Sirens recognize their own. That's why Cora's comfortable with Mel and why Mel was comfortable talking to her alone. If you do turn, Cora might be the only one on the ship that *is* safe with you."

I started to panic at that. *What if I hurt someone?* I loved the Daughters like they were family, and the last thing I wanted to do was hurt anyone.

She pulled to a stop in front of the door, spinning around and taking in the panic on my face. "You're not going to hurt anyone. I promise we'll make sure of it. Trust me."

I did trust her, and it helped knowing that Cora was safe with me. Hells, if I did turn, she might like me better.

"You're going to be fine. You won her over once, you can do it again."

I put my hand on the door, pausing when she said, "Wait, take this." Tess handed me the green jar.

"What is it?"

"Healing ointment. Mel helped make it and said it should help with Cora's side. Mel checked the wound. She's been healing, but not at the normal rate that sirens normally do. We're hoping this will help it along."

I nodded, taking the ointment and opening the door. I entered and was startled to find the room was empty aside from Cora in her tub. Melody had already left, and now I was alone again with Cora. *No, not Cora,* I mentally corrected. *Coral the siren, who doesn't remember me, and I need to be careful around.*

That was going to take some getting used to.

# Chapter Thirty Nine
## Coral

My little huntress stood in front of the door, watching me appraisingly. I watched her with new eyes after having talked to Melody, looking for any signs she might be turning, but I didn't see any.

She moved toward me slowly. I watched her for signs of aggression, but she didn't seem to be threatening me.

She stopped just out of my reach, her hand moving like she wanted to touch me. I grinned at her, showing her my teeth. "If you want to keep those fingers, I'd suggest keeping them to yourself."

She frowned at that. "Cora," she said slowly.

I interrupted her. "It's Coral." I didn't know why she kept getting my name wrong, but it was pissing me off. Coral wasn't a hard name to remember, and seas knew it was everywhere. Surely even a surface-dweller like her knew about the coral reefs.

"Sorry, okay, um, Coral, the captain gave me some salve to help with your side."

I looked down at my wound. The edges were knitting together painfully slowly, but I wasn't sure how much I could trust the pirates when it came to healing. Even if they tried to help, their surface-dwelling salves might not be safe for me. Plus, the pirates weren't the ones offering it to me. The huntress was, and I knew I didn't trust her.

Things would have been so much easier if I had just let her drown. I should have. I had no idea why I had been moved by a hunter dying in front of me, woman or not. If there was something about her eyes, about her face, that had struck a chord in me, I was choosing to ignore it now.

She was still staring at me, and the silence I thought I wanted was grating on my nerves.

"Why would I let you touch me?" I finally bit out.

She reeled back slightly, like I had struck her. "I'm just trying to help," she said hesitantly.

"Just trying to help? Why should I believe a word you say? And if the pirates are allies of the sirens, why are you alive?"

"I–" she breathed. "I don't understand."

"Why are they tormenting me?"

She sighed. "They mean for you to keep an eye on me."

I rolled my eyes. "Some allies, leaving the hard work to me."

"They're worried I'll turn."

I was surprised to hear the truth from her.

"Whether or not you turn, you'll turn on them. Why they trust you not to in the first place, I don't understand, little huntress."

"I–what?"

"The way you've been watching me appraisingly, searching for any weapon in here, I know you'll slit my throat the first chance you get, and believe me, the feeling is mutual."

I bared my teeth at her, and she gulped, looking concerned. Good.

"I'm not a hunter. I'm a pirate," she said slowly.

"And I'm not a siren," I said deadpan. "I'm a harmless little Mer." I batted my eyelashes, flicking my tail in frustration. "A lie being pretty doesn't make it truth."

"You don't understand. I'm not your enemy."

"No," I said, "you don't understand. You may not be a threat, but you are assuredly my enemy. Anyone sharing a ship, sharing the waters with those slaughterers, the men who murdered my sisters, should meet a violent end. Sure, you're better to look at than the lot of them, but that doesn't change a thing. Those pretty lips will scream just as well when I taste your blood. Your lot dies loudly."

She shuddered, and I took my small victory in stride. "I'm no friend of the Saints."

"That doesn't make you a friend of the sirens, or of me."

"You don't understand," she said, shaking her head in frustration. "I'm a Daughter. I sail on this ship with Captain Tess and Mel."

I blew out a breath, a cross between a laugh and a huff of disbelief. "Likely story. You were on the hunters' ship wearing their robes when I found you."

"Look," she said, "I'm not a seas damned hunter. I was over there trying to steal from them," she said, frustration escalating into an anger that I found intriguing. Interestingly enough, my siren instincts still didn't take over. Even angry, the siren in me didn't see this woman as a threat. My instincts were wrong, though. She was a hunter, so of course she was a threat and a good liar.

"If that's true, why are you being held in here, too?"

"I already told you," she ground out. "They're worried I might turn, so they want us together, just in case." Under her breath, she said, "They probably want to make sure I turn on you first."

"You're not strong enough to hurt me."

She took a few quick steps toward me. I moved back, not sure what she thought she was going to do. I was faster and stronger than her.

Before I could blink, she pulled a piece of the net still overhanging the tub over my face. My hands shot up in surprise to push it off me. She grabbed my hands and looped some of the net's rope around them, binding them together. "What are you doing?" I yelled out as I tried to pull apart the rope. I was strong, but apparently she was good with rope.

I was so focused on getting my hands free and the net off my face that I didn't notice her attention had moved to my tail until it was too late. She grabbed the net under my tail and pulled it up. I yelped, thrashing out, but I was too tangled up in the net to fight hard. She pulled the net, drawing my tail toward my face, bundling me up.

Adding insult to injury, she hoisted me up, pulling me out of the tub. She released the net in the middle of the room, leaving me splayed out, flopping uselessly. "Very funny. Now put me back," I demanded.

I rolled over and saw she was grinning at me. "Who's strong now?"

As much as I loathed to admit it, it was impressive she could pull one over on me like that and lift me out of the water.

"You've made your point. Now put me back," I said again.

She pulled a green jar from her pocket and said, "Since I can't trust you to help yourself or let me help you while you're in the water, I think I'll keep you like this."

I couldn't believe her. I squirmed, trying to get the net off me, but before I could move more, she straddled me just below where skin met tail, close to my injured side. I stopped moving, worried I would get hurt if she moved the wrong way. "What are you doing?" I hissed.

Her eyes widened. "Am I hurting you?"

"No, but you should get off me before you do."

She let out a relieved breath. "I'm going to do this as quickly and painlessly as I can, but you need help, and this salve is going to help you."

She reached in, taking a scoop of the salve in her fingers, and said, "Now show me where it hurts."

"I'm fine. It doesn't hurt, get off me," I grunted, thrusting my tail into her, but she clung on, tightening her thighs around me.

The sensation wasn't unpleasant, and it pissed me off. "Get off me, huntress," I bit out.

"Not until I help. Now which side was it?" She twisted and ran her thumb down my right side, watching my face. She ran her thumb from the start of my tail up the line of scales that stopped at my chest. I shivered at the touch.

She pulled away instantly. "Did that hurt?"

I grimaced and shook my head. "Quit touching me for fun, it's on the other side."

She looked smug as she set down the salve jar and said, "If you had just told me that, you wouldn't have to deal with the unnecessary touching. I just want–" She stopped with a fierce intake of breath when her eyes landed on my wound. The scales had done what they could to protect and cover the gash in my side, but it was clear she hadn't missed it and even clearer she knew it was worse that I had been letting on. It wasn't fatal, and I would be fine, but it just wasn't healing at the rate I was used to without the helping hand of the sea and my sisters.

"I'm fine," I said, gasping when she prodded the gash with her thumb. "What's wrong with you?" I asked, trying to pull away.

"I'm sorry," she said, pulling her hand away quickly. "It's hard to tell what's wound and what's scale." She moved her hand back to my side, and I squirmed again, not wanting her hand near the gash.

"Stop moving or I might actually hurt you. Relax, I'm just trying to help."

"Why should I trust you?"

She paused, her hand hovering over my side, and said, "I know you don't think you have any reason to trust me, and I know this doesn't make sense, but you remind me of someone I care deeply about. Whether you believe it or not, I won't hurt you. I'm only trying to help your stubborn ass because it would hurt me to see you suffering. So, if you wouldn't mind staying still, the sooner I get the salve on you, the sooner I can get this net off you and get you back in the water."

She was right. None of it made sense, but I couldn't sense any deceit or feel any danger in her intentions, so I stilled. I didn't want to be on the floor a minute longer than necessary.

I sucked in a breath as she stroked the salve over the gash in my side. The salve was cool to the touch. She immediately paused. "Everything okay?"

"Fine," I gritted out. "Hurry up."

She carefully spread the salve on the rest of the gash, her fingers trailing up my scales, higher than necessary, toward my chest. Pleasure shot through me at the feeling of her caress on my scales before I remembered myself. "You got all of it. Get your hands off me."

She immediately pulled her hands away, her face going red. "I'm sorry, I just wanted to be thorough. With the scales, it's hard to tell where it started and ended."

I begrudgingly nodded. As much as I disliked her, she was telling the truth. If I couldn't feel the gash with my every breath, I wasn't sure I would know how big it was either.

She shifted off me carefully and a sense of loss shot through me at not having her weight on top of me. I immediately pushed it from my mind. Whatever the little huntress was doing to me, it was stopping here and now.

"Okay," she said apologetically, "I didn't really think this through. I'm going to have to bundle you in the net again to move you back."

That was going to hurt my side a lot, being folded over like that.

She winced, seeming to come to the same realization before brightening. "Wait, if you let me, I can put a hand under your tail and your back and pick you up like that. Is that okay?"

I was surprised she had asked. I considered asking her to unbind my hands, but even if she did that, I couldn't get myself back into the tub without her help. Besides, I was feeling my scales start to dry and I couldn't decide if the itching was my imagination or if I was starting to turn into a human form. I didn't want to find out. I wasn't about to try out legs and be more at the mercy of my little huntress. "Fine, just do it quick."

She scooped her arms underneath me and hoisted me up in her arms with surprising ease and carried me the small distance to the tub, gently lowering me down into the water.

I sighed in relief as the water surrounded me, welcoming me back, and the itchiness of my scales disappeared immediately.

I popped my head back above the water and saw her waiting expectantly. I thrust my hands out to her, and she made quick work of undoing the net bindings. When it was off me, I went to throw it out of the tub before thinking better of it. It was the only thing I had and, if need be, it was my only potential weapon.

I pulled it under the water with me. I watched as my little huntress made her way back into her corner and gave me a little smile before she blew out the lantern and laid down in her makeshift nest.

I wondered if she knew I could still see her perfectly. I saw a sleepy little smile come over her face that was hard to hate, so I dropped back into the water, wanting her out of my sight.

I let my mind wander like I always did when my sisters found sleep and I couldn't. The moonlight leaking through the porthole and sparkling over my water made me feel a little more at home.

I pulled the net towards me and, without thinking much about it, draped it around myself, finding the weight comforting. I stretched out, looking at my side. I was surprised to find that the gash was a little more closed than before. Maybe the pirates weren't all that bad at healing after all.

I still didn't understand why the huntress had cared enough to help me, but I felt better than I had since I was first hit so I couldn't complain.

When sleep claimed me, those seaweed green eyes and helping hands entered my dreams against my will.

# CHAPTER FORTY
# Ray

I woke suddenly to the loud bang of the door and saw Scyla bursting her way in, followed closely by Addie with a tray of food, and then by an exasperated-looking Neta. By the light in the room, I guessed it was midday.

"I told you guys you aren't supposed to be in here. Captain's orders," Neta said, clearly frustrated.

"And I told you that Tess only said we couldn't touch or get within reach of either of them. She didn't say anything about seeing them." Scyla shot me a wink.

I laughed at that. I was sure Tess was trying to avoid all contact, even sight, but I couldn't help being glad Scyla hadn't listened.

"Besides," Addie piped up, "I'm sure we're not supposed to starve them. Come on, we'll leave in a little bit, pirate's honor."

"Pirates have no honor," Scyla said with a chuckle.

Addie chuckled too before asking, "Whose side are you on, anyway?"

"Please?" I turned, asking Neta, having figured out she had likely been given the job of guarding our door and keeping Scyla out. I felt sorry for her for being given such an impossible task.

If I were a good friend to her right now, I would tell them to listen to Neta and, by extension, to Tess, but I had missed them too much to ask them to leave.

I looked over and saw that Coral was awake too, watching them with mild interest.

Neta huffed out a breath. "Fine, but don't get too close or I really will have to kick you out."

"Thank you, thank you, thank you!" I squealed out.

Addie and Scyla grinned at me.

"I really missed you guys."

I heard a grunt from the tub and turned in her direction. Coral had propped her head on the edge, resting it on her folded arms. "And here I thought we were starting to be friends."

Scyla immediately turned her attention to the tub and my siren. *Well,* the *siren,* I amended as soon as the thought crossed my mind. Cora might've been mine, but Coral wasn't. The sooner I came to terms with that, the better. It was just so damn hard having her so close, returned to me, but not. This siren didn't trust me in the slightest, didn't know me, and didn't seem to care to.

Even at the beginning, before Cora and I became an *us,* before she got to know and trust me, she was always kind. My Cora didn't have a suspicious bone in her body. I loved her for it as much as it frustrated me. She had trusted the Saints, never really believing my 'wild theories' about them. Whatever had happened to her, whatever she remembered about the transformation had been enough to change all that. She hated me because she thought I was one of them.

I wasn't, but I wasn't wholly innocent, either.

I had saved myself from the Saints, but I hadn't done it quick enough to save her and I hated myself for that. I failed to protect her, and if having the hatred of Coral the siren was my punishment for failing to save my Cora, I would gladly pay that price for the miracle of seeing her still breathing. Whatever those monsters did to her, I would make them pay, too. The Saints hadn't seen the last of me.

It hurt when Coral looked at Scyla with curiosity but a noted lack of suspicion. It was the closest I had seen her looking like the version of her I had known, and it made my heart crack a little to know she was still in there.

Scyla looked at me, but I was watching Addie, who gave a little wave to Coral, who was now watching her. Addie turned to me with a small smile and asked, "Is this...?" She let her question trail off, but I knew what she was asking. I nodded.

"Aren't you going to introduce us?" Coral asked. "I didn't know the hunters lacked manners as well as humanity."

I was used to the barb, but the others looked surprised.

"The hunters?" Addie asked.

"It's what they call the White Robes," Scyla explained, before turning back to me to ask the obvious, "but why does she think you're one of them?"

"She was on their ship, in their dress, and wasn't scared about being there," Coral piped up, saving me the trouble of giving the answer I didn't fully understand myself. "We've never found a willing woman on the hunters' ships until *her*," she said with venom in her voice. "What they do to us is cold-blooded murder. What they do to their own, to their women, is worse."

"She's not one of them," Addie said.

"She's not, she's a pirate," Neta spoke up from near the door. It warmed my heart that she spoke up in my defense. A true Convent brat, she didn't waste words she considered unnecessary. I shot her a grateful smile. She nodded back, her lips quirking up in a motion so subtle I could have imagined it.

Scyla had been watching Coral and saw the same thing I did–that she wasn't convinced. "She's as pirate as they come," Scyla said again.

"So, what was she doing there?" Coral asked with narrowed eyes.

It wasn't an easily answered question. I had been there to avenge her death. I wasn't sure how to explain that and very much doubted she would believe the story that sounded unbelievable even to me, despite me having lived it.

Before Scyla could say anything, I said, "They stole something from me, so I paid them a little visit."

Scyla quirked an eyebrow at me in question. I just shrugged.

"Did you get it back?" Coral asked.

I chuckled at that. "In a way."

The others were watching us, but Scyla lost the fight against holding her own tongue and said, "I was there too, though, why aren't you suspicious of me?"

Coral looked her up and down and asked skeptically, "Should I be?"

Addie huffed out a laugh. "Of course not."

Scyla whirled on her. "Hey! I can be plenty dangerous. I'm scary and incredibly suspicious."

Addie met my eye and we both burst into giggles. Scyla was too easy to rile up.

Scyla glared at me. "Hey! I'm on your side here."

I put my hands up in defense. "I know, I know. You're plenty dangerous."

"And?" she prompted.

"And what?" I asked.

She looked at me pointedly. "And scary and suspicious."

She was, of course, rivaled in ferocity only by Captain Tess herself and maybe by Mel, but I didn't know enough of Mel's true strength to say, but it was too entertaining to mess with her like she often did to me.

"Um–" I looked at Neta who chuckled, then Addie, who looked away, and then back to Scyla. "Sure, so scary."

"You're a shit liar," she said.

"I said you were dangerous," I said, defending myself.

"Well, yeah, because you're a shit liar and can't deny I'm dangerous."

I laughed at that.

She turned to Addie, "Ads, I'm scary, right?"

Addie blinked, a moment of indecision passing over her face before she threw up her hands. "I adore you. You're a lot of things, but you're too transparent to be suspicious."

Scyla crossed her arms. "Good friends would've lied."

"I tried!" I chimed in.

She rolled her eyes. "Convincingly," she finished. "Good friends would have lied *convincingly*."

"It's hardly a bad thing," Neta said. Scyla didn't acknowledge that and turned back to Coral. "You're honestly saying Ray's scarier than me?"

That wasn't what she was saying though, and we all knew it. I watched Coral, waiting for her to correct Scyla. Instead, she nodded.

My jaw hit the floor.

Scyla was all toned muscle, while I barely had any weight to me. The other pirates sometimes joked that a stiff breeze could send me overboard. They weren't wrong. I was building more muscle the longer I sailed with them, but there was no doubt that Scyla was the stronger, more intimidating between us. There was no comparison. Scyla had taught me almost everything I knew; she was the dangerous one. She was an expert with a sword and an artist with a dagger.

"Why?" I choked out.

Coral turned, locking eyes with me. "The other one was scared."

"What?" I asked alongside a chorus of similarly confused sounds from my friends.

"She was on the hunters' ship, but she was scared. She was the reason we came. The Goddess was answering *her* need, not yours."

"I wasn't scared!" Scyla protested immediately. I almost believed her. I did believe she would've fought like the hells were at her back, and I was sure she would've taken some of the Saints there with her, but I couldn't imagine she was delusional enough to have thought she was getting out alive on her own, or even with my help. We both would've been dead without the fear that sent the sirens.

"But I was scared," I said.

"You weren't," Coral said in a way that made it clear she wouldn't put up with being argued with.

I considered her words, really thought about them, and tried to remember. When I set out on the mission, I was determined, not scared. I felt worried when Scyla insisted on joining, but I focused on reworking the plan to accommodate her instead of letting myself be scared. When I heard her cry out, I was too busy running plans to help her and get her back to be scared. Fear was a luxury I hadn't had time for.

Even when I was fighting Captain Butcher, Scyla was out of danger and I was focused on getting off the ship myself. I had made peace with my own death and wasn't scared of it. In that moment, with Scyla out of danger, I didn't truly care if I lived or died as long as it was quick. I knew the longer I stayed there alive on their ship, the longer I was putting my sisters and the sirens at risk.

"I guess I just didn't have time to be," I protested, looking around at the others, finding Scyla first, who was watching with a stunned look on her face.

"You–" she started before stopping and trying again, "You–didn't have time? To be scared...?"

The others looked at me with confusion, except for Coral, who still looked at me with mistrust, but there was some intrigue in her gaze that I hadn't noticed before.

I shrugged. "I had a job to do. I didn't expect to make it out alive, so it was a pleasant surprise."

Neta let out of huff that had me turning toward her. She raised her eyebrows at me, and Addie just continued to stare. Unsurprisingly, Scyla broke the silence with a laugh and clapped me on the back. "Only you would call living a pleasant surprise."

Neta stepped toward us, clearing her throat. Scyla and I remembered simultaneously that we weren't supposed to be touching and broke apart.

I missed the closeness the moment she moved, but if there was even a small chance that Tess and Mel were right to be worried about me, then it was better to be cautious.

I didn't feel different, though. I still felt like myself. I hoped they wouldn't keep me isolated for much longer. I was sure I wasn't going to turn–well, mostly sure anyway–and I missed the others.

"Enough talking for now, though," Scyla said. "I'm sure our guest is hungry."

I blinked, surprised for a moment, before remembering what was usually easy to forget; Scyla was Tess's first mate. She was always bossy, but I often forgot she had a right to be. She usually wasn't wrong though and it should've occurred to me far sooner that Coral likely hadn't eaten much last time either.

"Where are my manners?" Scyla said, turning back to Coral, "I'm Scyla, first mate to Captain Tess, who you've met."

Coral cocked her head to the side. "I thought Melody was her mate?"

We did our best to hold in our laughter as Scyla sputtered out, "Not like that."

"Melody and Captain Tess are lovers," Addie explained. "Scyla is Captain Tess's second in command on the ship."

Scyla nodded gratefully to Addie, and turned back to Coral. "And this is Adeline,"

"Addie for short," Addie interjected. Looking at Coral, she explained, "My friends call me Addie."

"And you expect we'll become friends?" Coral asked.

"I do," Addie said with a grin.

"I admire your confidence, misplaced as it is," Coral said with a hint of a smile that made my heart race. It instantly became my new mission to get her to smile like that at me. I reminded myself again that somewhere in there, she was still my Cora. I had won her over once without even trying; I had to believe I could do it again.

"And this is Ant–" Scyla started but was interrupted by an elbow to the gut. Scyla grunted, bending over with the force.

"Neta, it's Neta."

I had figured out after a long while of sailing with them that Neta was short for Antoniette. I knew of her at the Convent. We hadn't been friends, but I had heard when she was called from the Convent by the sea for her sins. I hadn't bothered asking why she kept her name to herself now. To us Convent brats, nicknames weren't about preference now, but protection.

Of course, Neta was safe with us and with Coral. The siren didn't have anyone to tell, anyway. But Neta was a special case. Scyla had explained to me that Neta went by her new name now because it was what her sister used to call her, and it was her way of keeping her sister close.

Since Scyla herself didn't go by her full name, Priscyla, I figured she would understand.

She paled and quickly corrected, "Sorry Neta, won't happen again."

"If it does, I'll start calling you Pris."

That immediately broke any rising tension in the room and Neta held out her hand and pulled Scyla back up straight. It seemed the troubled seas were behind us.

Scyla turned back to Coral. "And you know Ray" she said. I noticed she purposefully used my nickname and wasn't sure if that was for Neta's benefit or Coral's. She was likely trying to show Neta she was trying to understand us Convent brats, but I wanted Coral to hear my full name.

"Ray's short for Rayana." My heart soared when a small flash of confused recognition flitted across her face, but it was gone just as soon as it came.

"Coral," she said carefully, "long for Cor, the only part of my old life I remembered to keep when the Goddess granted me a new one."

I took in the new information, allowing a little spark of hope at the knowledge that she remembered something. Sure, it was only a part of her name, but she remembered it. If she could remember that, there was hope she could remember other things, too.

Scyla took some food for her, Addie, and Neta and passed the tray to me. I took some jerky and an orange and left the rest for Coral. I was surprised to see she didn't hesitate to help herself, unlike last time.

Coral was mostly quiet as the rest of us ate and talked. I missed them all so much and couldn't wait to get out of here. Of course, my freedom would mean Coral's too, which was hard to be excited about. I loved Cora and wanted her safe and happy more than anything, at any cost. I had just never imagined that her happiness would take her away from me.

She wasn't gone yet, though. I still had time to win her back.

# Chapter Forty One
# Ray

I was still catching up with Scyla and Addie when the door opened again and Tess and Mel came in. Neta jumped up from where she was sitting by the door and started to say something, but Tess cut her off. "Please don't worry, I know Scyla well enough to know she wouldn't listen. I *am* impressed you managed to keep everyone besides her and Addie out, though."

Neta relaxed at that, and I felt my own shoulders slump in relief.

"I would hope to be invited the next time you throw a party though," she said, looking at Scyla who just laughed.

"Wouldn't be much of a rule-breaking secret party if I invited the rule maker."

"Hardly a secret," Tess said grinning, causing Scyla to pout a moment before Tess continued, "Okay fine, it wasn't the first place I looked for you."

Scyla grinned at that until Mel added, "It was the second."

We all laughed at Scyla's scowl.

"Look I don't mind the two of you visiting if you're careful, but we don't want anyone else getting in here," Tess explained, looking at me apologetically. "You're coming out of the danger zone, but we have to be careful for a little bit longer."

"I understand. It's okay," I reassured her, and it really was. I didn't mind being stuck in here with Coral. Knowing she was leaving soon, that

I was going to lose her again when I had only just found her, made me want to spend every spare second with her if she would let me.

"Thank you," she said with a smile, before turning to the others. "We do need you all out now, though. Mel and I have to talk to our guest."

Scyla took one look between Tess and Mel before nodding and clearing out with Addie. It shouldn't have surprised me. Scyla had been with the crew far longer than I had and had earned her spot at Tess's side. I knew she must listen to her sometimes to merit the position as number two but seeing her actually defer to Tess was still surprising.

Not nearly as surprising as Mel's request was, though.

"You want me to do what?" Coral sputtered out.

They wanted her to test out her legs. I couldn't even begin to imagine what it would be like seeing the siren Coral walking on two legs, the siren Coral without a tail and the closest to Cora that she had been since I had found her again.

"We think it might be good for you to give it a try."

"But I can't," she said, shaking her head quickly. "If you wanted what was good for me, you'll throw me back in the water and be done with it."

Tess and Mel exchanged a look and Mel said, "I know it's a scary thought. I've been there, I understand."

"I don't see you splashing around here with a tail. If it's so easy transforming, why don't you?"

Mel looked like Coral had struck her and Tess took a half step in front of her, an anger I had never seen before blazing in her eyes. I found myself shifting infinitesimally between her and Coral.

"Do you think it would help with the healing?" I asked Mel.

Tess came back to herself with a blink and moved slightly out of Mel's way.

"The transformation magic that changes the body could help close the wound," Mel said hesitantly.

"Or it could make it worse," Coral grumbled.

"Could it?" I asked.

Mel sighed. "It's possible, but it's more likely to help."

"I don't know if I can," Coral said carefully.

"I'm sure you can. You're strong," I said quickly.

She narrowed her eyes at me. "You're just as scared as I am of the transformation."

She wasn't wrong. I tried not to think about it because there wasn't anything to be done about it, but she was right. I was scared.

I started to say so, but Coral had a glint in her eye that stole my speech as a smile spread across her lips. "I know you're scared. Don't bother denying it."

She looked back at Tess. "A compromise. I'll try if she does."

I gulped.

"She can't!" Tess insisted, looking at Mel for back up but Mel shrugged.

"It might be good to figure out once and for all if there's anything to be worried about. They can swap places and we'll keep an eye on–"

"No," Coral interrupted.

"What?" Mel asked, confusion on her face.

"No, the transformation is intimate. I won't try it with anyone watching, and I won't try unless she does first," she said, nodding in my direction.

Tess and Mel exchanged looks, and it was easy to tell they didn't like it. I expected Tess to shut it down immediately, but instead Mel asked me, "What do you think?"

My first instinct was to say yes, but I forced myself to actually consider it. I didn't believe I would turn. If I was going to, I was sure it would've happened by now, but what if I was wrong? Even with Mel's expertise, there was so much we didn't understand about the transformation. Was I willing to risk my life as I knew it?

"Where would I do it?" I asked.

Mel's eyes widened fractionally as she considered. "We could bring in another tub."

"There's room in here," Coral supplied with a flick of her tail.

We all stared at her.

"You want me in there with you?"

"It hardly matters what I want, but it's practical. If you turn, it'd be better for me to be close."

"It's too risky," Tess argued.

"Don't trust me?" Coral asked, looking directly at me, a challenge in her eyes. This was it. This was the moment of no return. If I backed down, I would lose her for sure. She had extended this offer of peace, and I could either be brave and seize it or let it pass me by. But I was done letting life pass me by.

"I'll do it."

# CHAPTER FORTY TWO
## Coral

Funny Hat and the land siren bickered with the huntress, but it hardly mattered. The huntress had made up her mind, and they weren't going to get her to back down now.

They finally left, leaving me alone again with the huntress, but the energy had shifted. I wasn't sure what I believed about her anymore, but she had convinced me she at least didn't want to hurt me.

She had helped me. The salve had made a world of difference, and the pirates claimed her as a friend. Whatever she was, they trusted her. Since Charia trusted the pirates, and even I couldn't deny they had been as kind to me as they could, it made me question myself.

Maybe I was wrong about her, and if I wasn't, I'd be able to drown her before she could hurt me.

The huntress closed the door behind the pirates and turned back to me. I watched her as she cautiously walked towards me. She stopped halfway across the room, just watching me.

"Well?" I asked.

She startled at that. "Well what?"

"Are you getting in? Water's nice and warm." I flicked my tail, pushing a little water in her direction and laughed when she jumped out of the way. Then I noticed her face actually held a trace of fear that I had never seen on her. She hadn't shown fear when I had tried to drown her or when she was dying in the sea, but she was afraid now.

"Hey," I said carefully, "you're okay. I'm right here."

She relaxed at that a lot more than I expected and I couldn't help but add, "I'm the only thing here you need to fear."

She smiled a little at that, "I suppose a little water isn't nearly as scary as you."

I grinned back. "Exactly. What do you have to fear?"

"Promise you won't try to drown me again?"

I thought about being snarky, but it was undeniable that something had changed between us, and it didn't feel right to make things worse when she was already eyeing the water with fear. "There are far better uses for beautiful women than drowning."

Her eyes snapped from the water up to mine. "You think I'm beautiful?"

I had meant to distract her. Apparently, it worked too well.

"I do have eyes, and I might be dangerous, but I'm not a liar."

She smiled at that and moved a little closer.

I couldn't stop myself from adding, "Why don't you come a little closer and I'll show you just what I think of you?"

She paused at that, and I saw the hesitation in her eyes. I wasn't going to hurt her. I was as interested as Funny Hat and Melody were to see if she would actually transform. I was hardly an expert on being a siren. In fact, I was positive that Melody knew more than I did, and maybe more than Charia, too. I wanted to see what would happen.

Melody was sure that if she did turn, I would hold some sort of sway over the huntress, though, and I was dying to know what that would be like. It hardly mattered, of course, because I was sure she wasn't going to transform, but I couldn't help but picture what it would be like to have her with a tail and scales. Her blond hair fanned out as she writhed under me, as I kissed my way down from her neck to the scales at her chest.

I shook the thoughts away. They had come out of nowhere and weren't helping me stay focused on the scared girl in front of me.

I could try to lure her to me, but I wasn't sure if it would work. It didn't normally with women. Besides, it felt important that this was her choice since she would have to live with the consequences. If she did turn, I wouldn't be upset about it, but she likely would be.

I had no idea what it would be like for her to have had such a slow transition. I didn't know if she would remember anything or how she would feel about it, so this needed to be her choice.

"I won't force you but having you closer wouldn't be the worst."

She took a couple of steps closer and hesitated, fingering her coat. "Should I?"

I shrugged. "Do you normally swim in all that?"

She chuckled. "Obviously not."

"Well..."

"Well?"

"Probably best to take it off then. Wouldn't want anyone to say you weren't committed."

She watched me carefully as she pushed her coat off. It hit the floor with a thud, leaving her standing there in a loose white shirt with a tight-looking corset and tighter pants. She leaned over and tugged off her boots.

She was still mostly covered. "Is that it?"

She looked down. "Are you saying I should take off more?"

I shrugged. "I'm saying it'd hardly be practical not to."

She reached behind her back, and I watched for a few moments while she tried to fuss with the strings. She huffed out a frustrated sigh before I let myself laugh and said, "Get over here."

She looked surprised for a moment. "You remember how to take off a corset?"

*How hard could it be to help a beautiful woman undress?* "I'll manage."

She turned her back to me and moved to the side. I took up the strings and, much to my relief, found it was a lot like untangling a fishing net. I had it off of her in no time.

"Should I?" she asked, gesturing to her skin-tight pants.

I nodded, and she pulled those off too, leaving her standing there in just her draping white shirt.

She put her hand on the tub, and I held my hand out to her. She put her other hand in mine and swung her leg over the lip of the tub. I shifted my tail slightly, giving her a place to put her foot. I looked up at her, watching her steady herself, monitoring her face for any sign of discomfort but saw none. So far so good. I was incredibly tempted to shift my tail into her foot and knock her the rest of the way down, but she didn't look entirely calm yet.

She bent her other leg and pulled it into the tub with us. She carefully put it down in the only space my tail left for her. Apparently, I had overestimated how much room there actually was in here. My tail didn't leave much room for her. She let go of my hand and moved her foot a little further back, brushing against my tail, causing my entire body to shiver at the contact, knocking her off balance. She collapsed into me, falling on top of me and knocking the wind out of us both.

I reached out to steady her, my hands on her upper arms as they found their way around me.

As she had with the salve, her legs were on either side of my tail, pressed tightly against me since there wasn't room for them to be further away. Like with the salve, I felt a warmth spread at her touch, but things were different now. For one, we had formed something of a truce, and secondly, there wasn't a net restraining me this time.

There was nothing holding me back from touching, caressing the pretty little huntress who was lying on my chest. She was heaving deep breaths, eyes wide, and–seas take me, I wanted her.

I leaned toward her, waiting to see if she would stop me, but she didn't move. I was a breath away from her lips, and still, she didn't move. I knew with a flick of my tail I could close the distance. She hadn't moved, so she must have wanted this too.

It was that thought that stopped me.

If she wanted this, I would make her take it. I wasn't going to make things easy for her. I moved my lips to her jaw and planted kisses up her jaw to her ear. I grazed my teeth over her ear, making her cry out.

"Something wrong?" I asked.

She shook her head.

"Something feel weird?" I asked, moving my tail under her legs.

She moaned, tightening her thighs around me, making my breath hitch. I ran my hands up the sides of her white, now transparent shirt. It was a pointless piece of teasing fabric that I wanted to tear off her, but I let it stay. If she wanted more, she was going to have to take it.

I brushed my hand against the underside of her breast and heard her moan.

"Goddess save me," she groaned as she closed the gap and kissed me.

Seas help me, I was lost. I could have drowned in her kiss.

I pulled her closer, moving back to give us more room. She pulled me closer. I didn't notice until she gasped into my mouth that I had dragged her underwater with me.

I loosened my grip on her, but to my surprise, she didn't pull away. She pressed closer and kept kissing me. I wanted to see her writhing under me, but I didn't dare move her. Now that I was coming around to her, I had no desire to accidentally drown her.

Not that she wasn't trying herself. She had been underwater longer than most surface dwellers could and had to be running out of air. I pushed her gently to the surface. If she wasn't going to care for herself, I was going to have to.

When I breached the surface with her, she groaned and pushed back into me. "I could've lasted longer."

I laughed at that and turned her over, putting her back to me, cradling her against me. "Let's get a look at you. How are you feeling?"

She gasped, and I followed her gaze to her still very human legs. "I'm fine, I don't have a tail."

"A pity," I joked.

She smiled a little, but I sensed the tension in her and quickly amended, "Seas, you're beautiful now. You with a tail would be torturous."

She gave a true smile at that, and I tightened my grip on her. My little huntress was seas damned adorable. She settled into me and my heart melted at the level of trust she gave that I very clearly hadn't earned. I didn't know which of us was the dangerous one anymore, but I knew the time had passed where I was a danger to her. I would do dangerous things for her, but never to her.

"So, the danger of transforming has passed," I said softly.

"Do you think?"

I did. I didn't know everything there was to know about the transformation, but she had been immersed and hadn't changed. If she were going to, she would have by now, but I had only agreed to stay long enough to watch her. If she was fine, then I could and likely should be leaving. If I was sure she was fine, I had no reason to stay.

Instead, I said, "I can't be sure, of course, maybe a few more days to be safe."

The tension in her shoulders eased. "I think you're right."

We heard the door open, and I wondered if she would move away from me, but she didn't.

"How's it going in here?" Melody asked, breaking into a full grin when she saw us together.

"Still human?" Funny Hat asked from behind her.

"As human as ever," my huntress said, grinning from my arms.

"And I'm still as monstrous as ever," I said with a grin and was rewarded with my huntress chuckling in my arms.

"Yes, don't worry, I haven't tamed her. If anything, she's attempting to tame me."

"So, one experiment down," Melody said carefully, meeting my eye before continuing, "What do you think about giving legs a try?"

"Will it hurt?" I asked her.

I didn't want to, but my huntress had braved the water for me. It might not be terrible giving legs a try. I had lived a whole life with them before, and it might be worth trying again. Clearly Melody liked the experience enough to stay on land.

"It's a little uncomfortable at first, but you get used to it."

I wasn't sure if I would, but I had already agreed. "Fine, I'll try, but I might hate it."

"If you do, you don't have to try again. I just wish some of our sisters would give it a shot."

It was the loneliness with a sliver of hope in her eyes that convinced me. Land siren or not, sirens were sisters, and my sister wanted a friend. I couldn't say no.

# CHAPTER FORTY THREE
## Coral

I was laid out on the ground wrapped up in the sail my huntress had been using to sleep. I had laid there for a minute, waiting for something to happen, but nothing had.

Melody, Funny Hat, and my huntress were all staring down at me, watching and waiting expectantly.

After another silent moment, I asked, "Is something supposed to be happening?"

Melody frowned, "Are you dry yet?"

I flicked my tail, "Damp but definitely not wet,"

"May I?" she asked as she approached me. I wasn't sure what she was going to do, but I nodded.

She pulled the sail tight around me and started to rub my tail. The fabric felt coarse against my scales and started to chafe and itch. I squirmed, and she stopped. "What are you feeling?"

"Itchy."

She grinned, turning to the others. "It's working! Any second now."

To my dismay, she turned back to me and kept rubbing my tail dry. The discomfort rose to just shy of pain when I felt something snap and all of a sudden my tail felt like it had sprung apart. I cried out in alarm, but was thrilled to find the itching had stopped.

I looked down and tried to move my tail, the movement disturbed the bottom of the sail and I was shocked to see that where my tail had been, there were now feet poking out of the sail.

"I have legs," I whispered.

Melody cried out, "It worked!"

Funny Hat and my huntress just stared openmouthed at me.

I wiggled my toes, testing them.

Melody straightened up and held out her hand to me. I took it but didn't know what to do.

"Don't just stand there," she said to the others, "help her up!"

My huntress immediately grabbed my other hand, and they yanked me up. I was graceful in the water, but apparently that didn't translate to being on land. I was only standing on my legs for a moment before I started to topple forward. My huntress stepped in front of me, blocking my fall as I fell into her chest instead of onto the floor.

"Easy there," she said softly.

I looked over and saw that Melody was trying not to laugh. When she saw I was watching her, she quickly said, "You're doing great! I wasn't much better my first time, either. It'll get easier."

With my huntress's stabilizing arms around me, I felt like Melody had to be right. I was already standing tall until the rest of her words registered. Just how often did she think I planned to do this for it to get easier?

I wasn't sticking around. They knew that. In another few days, I was out of here. In another few days, I was going to rejoin my sisters in the sea. I should have been ecstatic about that, but it was hard to feel happy about the thought of not seeing my huntress again when I was in her arms, when I had tasted her lips. Whatever magic she had done to me, it was working. I was feeling more lost than I could ever remember feeling.

# Chapter Forty Four
## Ray

When Coral was steadier, I loosened my grip on her and gave her over into Mel's care. She was asking Mel questions about the transformation and about her new legs, but I was having a hard time listening. I knew that, tail or not, this was still Coral the siren, but it was harder to remember that when she was standing there on two legs in front of me. Harder to remember that even though she had kissed me, this wasn't my Cora. I wanted to tell her everything, to try to remind her about what we were to each other, but I didn't think it would do me any good. I could see she was warming up to me, and I worried that that would break the fragile trust I was building with her.

Or maybe not telling her would be the thing that broke us. Maybe by not telling her, she would leave, and I would never see her again. It was a reality I was trying to prepare myself for, but the longer I spent with her, the harder I knew it was going to be to see her leave.

"She still doesn't remember?" Tess asked softly after they had left.

I shook my head. "I thought she might after the kiss," I admitted. A foolish, romantic part of me thought that kissing her might break whatever hold the magic had on her. True love's kiss was supposed to be able to shatter most magic. Either that didn't extend to the sea, or I wasn't her true love. Either way, I was struggling to face the reality that even on legs, she was lost to me.

Coral was feisty and beautiful, but she wasn't my Cora. Maybe with more time for her to let her guard down, she could be, but it didn't change the fact that she didn't have any of the memories I did. She didn't remember anything about us. Her only memories of her previous life were ones of pain, and I didn't know if she would ever find her way back to who she was, and it wasn't fair of me to want her to.

I could grow to love this version of her, but I was starting to doubt if she could feel the same. It was starting to become clear just how selfish I was being. Even if she had started to feel something for me, she wasn't happy here. She had a new family below the waves. She was a siren, and I was just the lovesick pirate who couldn't let her go. I had joined the Daughters hoping to find her, but if I had been more honest, I hadn't really expected to succeed. I had really been looking for peace, for closure, and in a weird way through finding her, I had found it. "I don't know if she ever will remember."

Tess put her hand on my shoulder. "It's not too late. You don't have to give up yet."

I sighed. I wanted to believe that things would find a way to work out, but I was starting to think that this was the divine plan for us. That we were both on our own paths, and she had crossed mine one last time for a final goodbye.

"I know I don't have to, but she deserves to be free. I think we should let her go."

I knew what that meant, knew that it would be the last time I saw her, but I couldn't keep holding onto the past and I couldn't keep holding her back.

"Are you sure?" Tess asked.

I nodded, sure I was going to regret it the moment she was gone, but I knew I was doing the right thing. "I can't keep chasing the past."

# CHAPTER FORTY FIVE
# Coral

It was slow going at first, but Melody was right there supporting me, and I was surprised to find she was right. After a few minutes, my body started to adjust, and my legs didn't feel nearly as foreign as they had at first.

"You're getting the hang of it," she said with a smile.

I had to agree. A few more steps and she moved her arm from my back. I panicked for a moment, but a muscle memory I didn't understand kicked in and I found I was able to walk without her support.

"Maybe it's not that hard after all."

She grinned at me, "You know, the surface isn't all that bad. I have a pretty great life here."

I tried to ignore why she would have felt the need to make that comment in the first place. Surely it was so I could carry the message to Charia that Melody was happy up here. That had to be it, because it couldn't be that she was commenting on me and the huntress. I didn't know how I felt about the huntress, but I knew whatever it was wasn't enough to change my nature. I was a siren; I was meant for the water with my sisters. If Melody could suppress that, that was one thing, but I couldn't. I wouldn't.

It didn't matter that my siren instincts had quieted while I was on the ship. I couldn't trust myself. I was a monster, and I wasn't safe around the surface dwellers, or rather, they weren't safe around me.

It would be better for everyone when I left. At least, that's what I kept telling myself. I tried to ignore the thoughts of the huntress's lips against mine and the pang of familiarity that had resonated in my heart when I held her against me.

It didn't matter; I didn't belong here.

"I can't stay, you know that."

"You mean you don't want to stay. You could if you wanted to. I did."

"That's different. You have your mate here."

She looked at me, eyebrows cocked, "you're not exactly alone here."

It was different.

"You're pretty cool for a land siren, but you can't replace the entire pod."

She sighed at that, "Not what I meant, but you're right. I can't, but maybe the pirates can, though. They did for me."

That stopped my thoughts in their tracks. I had known on some level of course that she was comfortable here and that she felt safe, but it hadn't occurred to me that she really felt like she belonged here, not just with her Captain but with the pirates too. She was one of them, even more than she was siren now.

"It's different. You belong here."

She turned to me and took my hands in hers, looking me in the eye when she said, "It doesn't have to be different. You could belong here, too."

Before I could say anything, we were interrupted by one of my huntress's pirate friends whirling around the corner. She careened into Melody, almost sending us toppling over, but by a miracle of the seas, my legs didn't buckle underneath me.

"Mel, where's Tess?" she blurted out.

"Scyla, what's–" Mel started to ask before realizing the urgency and said, "Back in storage with Ray, but–" Before the words even finished leaving Mel's mouth, Scyla had bounded past us toward my huntress and the Captain.

"What–?" Melody started, but I took her hand and pulled her behind Scyla's retreating form. Clearly, something was wrong.

I pushed my new legs faster than I had yet and was pleased to find they obeyed without objection.

We got back to my huntress and the Captain in time to hear that we had company, and then we were all careening toward the upper decks.

# CHAPTER FORTY SIX
# Ray

We had a siren visitor. In the entire time I had been sailing with the Daughters, I hadn't so much as heard a whisper of the sirens directly interacting with the pirates, and based on how Tess and Scyla were reacting, this clearly wasn't a common occurrence.

To my delighted surprise, Coral grabbed my hand as we rushed after the others. I told myself it was probably because she was still unsteady on her feet, but she seemed confident enough that she was pulling me along. I gave her a reassuring squeeze and waited to see if she would drop my hand, but she didn't.

When we got to the deck, the crew was hauling a lifeboat onto the deck. I went to join them, but Coral was still holding my hand. Before I could decide whether to disentangle myself, they got the boat onto the deck. It landed with a thud and a splash of water.

The lifeboat was filled with water and inside rested a white haired siren with a long pale grey tail. She had the look of a warrior, beautiful and terrifying. "Charia!" Coral said from my side. She immediately dropped my hand and rushed forward, enveloping the siren in a hug. It made me anxious having Coral in the arms of someone so clearly lethal, but the siren hugged her back tenderly in a way that had emotions bubbling to the surface. The way she looked at Coral was almost motherly.

"We missed you, little one," she said quietly.

"I missed you all too," she said sheepishly.

"What are you doing here?" Mel finally asked.

"I missed you too, my child," Charia said, smiling at Melody. "I should've come sooner, but the Goddess forced my hand now."

"What happened?" Mel asked, the color draining from her face.

Coral pulled back, letting go of Charia and I was surprised when she took a few steps back toward me. I crossed the rest of the distance, meeting her halfway. Sensing she might need me.

"It's Rezi. She's been taken."

Coral faltered on her feet, falling back into me, and I thanked the Goddess I was there to support her and keep her upright.

A hush fell over the ship, quiet enough to hear Mel's follow up question. "Alive?"

Charia nodded. "For now."

"How long ago?" Coral asked.

"Not long. She was on patrol and got too close. We couldn't get to her in time before they caught her in their nets. She left her bracelet there for us to find, so we know they took her alive. I didn't know what to do, so I came here."

"You did the right thing," Tess said quickly. "Where are they?"

"I can lead you to them."

"What ship?" Scyla asked.

"One of their bigger ones," Charia said, skirting answering the question.

"It's them, isn't it?" Coral said quietly enough I couldn't believe the other siren heard her.

She went rigid in my arms when Charia nodded.

"Goddess," Tess whispered.

Scyla nudged her in the side and said loudly, "By the seas, the Goddess is with us tonight."

Tess straightened up, picking up the cue. "The Goddess is giving us another chance." She turned to me and Coral and said, "You'll have your revenge tonight. We'll save a siren and show those heretics once and for all what it means to incur the wrath of the Daughters of the Deep. Let's send them to their gods."

A rallying cry rose through the crew as Tess started barking orders. A few of the crew hefted the lifeboat up and lowered the siren back to the water.

I held tightly to Coral, not trusting her legs to support her. I didn't want to let her out of my arms or my sight, but I knew I was being selfish, so when the other siren was halfway back to the water, I forced out the question, "Do you want to go with her?"

That startled her out of her daze. She tried to turn but found I was holding her too tight. I reluctantly loosened my grip, and she turned around to face me.

"Are you telling me to go?"

"Of course not!" I said immediately. "I'm asking if you want to. I'd rather you stayed. The last thing I want is for you to leave."

"I'd probably be more helpful in the water."

I knew she was right, but I didn't want her anywhere near the ship that had taken her.

"You don't have to go anywhere," I said quickly.

Mel approached us and asked, "What do you want to do?"

I wasn't sure if she was talking to me or Coral, and it appeared Coral wasn't either since we both just stared at her.

"Are we staying or going with Charia?"

Coral sputtered out the question, "We?"

In all my time here, I had never seen Mel so much as look at the water, and here she was offering to dive into battle with Coral. I couldn't believe it and I was choking on how grateful I was.

I knew the others would protect Coral, but I didn't know them. Mel was family, and I knew with everything in me that she would protect Coral with her life.

"I'm not much help up here and I don't know how much help I would be down there, but whatever you want to do, I'm coming with you."

"But why? You have a life here."

"And you're starting to. I won't leave you to face down the heretics on your own. By land or by sea, I'll fight with you."

"But you haven't swum in so long."

"A siren never really loses her scales."

"Big talk for a land siren."

Mel laughed a loud musical laugh at that, "Land siren? Am I so washed up that that's what they call me?"

Coral was blushing and Goddess, was she beautiful.

"If you want to go, I'm coming."

I hoped for Mel's sake and my sanity that Coral didn't want to go. Mel was putting on a brave face, but I knew enough to know how much the offer was costing her. She hadn't turned in so long and feared losing herself to the transformation. She talked of uncontrollable urges that the sirens faced and fought off. Scyla had told me once that Mel was scared that if she turned, she wouldn't find her way back to us, back to Tess.

"We'll stay if someone shows me how to be useful here."

Mel and I exchanged relieved looks, and we rushed her below deck to get her outfitted for battle.

She wasn't nearly as hopeless as I expected. She wasn't surefooted, but she had maintained the quick reflexes and strength of her siren form.

I hoped it wouldn't come to up-close combat, but I was reasonably reassured she would be able to hold her own long enough to fend off an attacker until help arrived.

I didn't plan on being more than a couple feet from her the entire time but seeing that she was able to defend herself made me feel safer having her above deck with me. This was good because I was certain that if I tried to lock her up below deck, it would shatter the tentative trust we had built. I would have done it if I thought she would be in danger above, but I was glad her skills were passable enough I didn't have to.

# CHAPTER FORTY SEVEN
# Coral

Mel stayed with me and my huntress, suiting me up with heavy protective gear and weapons. I would have protested, but they both suited up similarly. I hated feeling like a liability, but thankfully they didn't seem all that worried about my skills. It was helping stave off the guilt I was feeling. I knew I would be of more help in the water, but something was telling me to stay here. I had grown to care for these pirates. I could easily see now why Melody and Charia wanted to protect them.

Returning to the water for this battle felt too much like abandoning them. Even my little huntress was growing on me, and the way she was clinging to me, I didn't feel right leaving her on her own.

When Melody made it clear that she would follow wherever I went, I knew I couldn't go. I couldn't force the land siren back into her scales. We would have to ride this one out together.

The ship lurched dangerously as we sped after the hunters. The ship was fast by itself, but this had my sisters written all over it. We were practically shoving our way through the waves. It made me smile even as we stumbled about on the deck. Melody and I stayed out of the way as the others ran around preparing and following the captain's orders.

"What happens when we catch up?" I asked her quietly.

"If we're quick enough, we'll launch a rescue."

She didn't have to explain why we were in a rush. We needed to get to Rezi before something worse happened. Since we were trained not to be taken alive, we had to get there quickly if we wanted any hope of saving her.

I couldn't stop myself from remembering how gentle and caring Rezi had been with me. She had spent the whole first night of my transformation with me, helping ease my discomfort, pain, and confusion. For a siren, she had a bleeding heart. She wouldn't survive the horrors the hunters would inflict on her, but they wouldn't survive the night if we had anything to say about it.

Mel took my hand and squeezed it. "We'll be quick enough."

I squeezed hers back. I wasn't sure if it was true, but I needed to believe it.

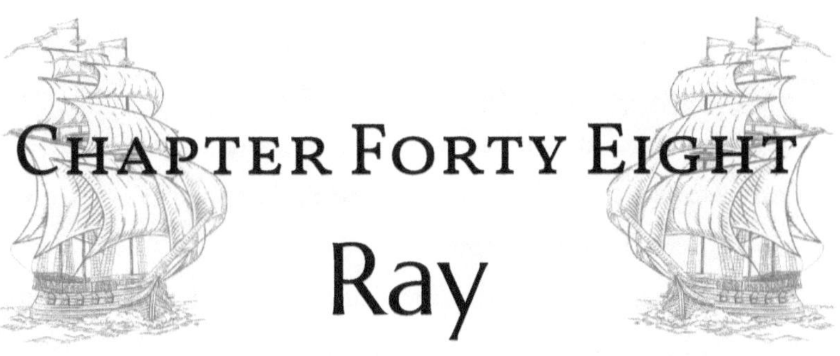

# Chapter Forty Eight

# Ray

The ship was in our sights. It was unmistakably the same ship that had nearly claimed my life just days ago, the same ship that stole Cora from me, and I couldn't help but think that the Goddess was giving us another shot at them.

I finished tying off the rigging I was working on and went looking for Coral and Mel. Tess was a damn good captain and knew I wouldn't be much use in a battle with Coral in danger, so my job was to make sure she and Mel stayed safe. I was relieved to be able to stay by Coral's side and was incredibly honored to have been trusted with Mel's safety, too.

I shouldn't have to do much. We weren't going to be boarded because we were launching an offensive, but on the off chance that any of the Saints made it onto our ship, no one would touch Mel or Coral on my watch.

They were both capable enough, but ideally, neither of them would need to prove that.

We were approaching the other ship fast and showing no signs of slowing.

"Ready yourselves," Tess screamed as we saw an incoming cannonball. It seems we had lost what little element of surprise we had.

The cannonball whirled harmlessly over the ship, but there would be others. We were closing the distance fast, and I braced for impact. The sirens were intent on getting their sister back, and it seemed like they were willing to sink both ships to accomplish that.

I grabbed Coral and pulled her to me, bracing us against the mast behind her as best I could, but we pulled up just shy of collision with a jolting force in the other direction.

I breathed a sigh of relief before realizing how they had positioned us. We were within rope's reach of the other ship.

Our crew was ready to go on the ropes and grappling hooks. Their whooping cries as they swung the gap to board the enemy ship mixed with the siren songs beginning below. Unfortunately, the men didn't seem swayed by the song. We already knew they had learned to plug their ears, but I had been hoping the sirens would be able to take out at least some of the men before word traveled aboard their own ship.

Addie called out orders to the rest of us, while Tess and Scyla led the charge on the enemy ship. I was surprised to see that Neta had joined the fray with the rest of the crew.

"What's Neta doing over there?" I asked Mel.

"We couldn't stop her."

"Wouldn't her arrows be more effective?"

Mel looked at me in surprise before understanding dawned on her face. "She didn't tell you?" she asked.

"Tell me what?"

"Rezi's her sister."

Well, shit.

Seas, how she had kept her composure was beyond me, but watching her cut her way through the men on the other ship between her and her sister–it made sense now.

I had been sure Neta was more deadly with her arrows, but she was piling the bodies up high enough to make me question that.

The second wave of our fighters swung over onto the ship now that the first wave had cleared some room for them. Half our crew and most of our best fighters were now on the other ship. The Saints had a bigger ship and outnumbered our crew, but there was only so much room above deck. The Saints were trying to rush out from belowdecks only to be cut down by waiting swords or tossed overboard into the arms of the sirens.

"They don't have Rezi yet," Coral breathed out, watching the other ship as intensely as I was.

Mel grabbed and squeezed Coral's shoulder. "They'll find her. We were quick enough."

I nodded. We had to have been quick enough because anything less was unacceptable.

There were bodies strewn all over the other ship now. Bile rose in my throat as I took in a few bodies with black pants and brown boots breaking up the sea of white fabric. I had known there might be casualties but knowing that and seeing it were very different things.

The remains of our crew had broken through enemy lines and Neta was first to shove herself below deck, followed closely by Tess and Scyla. They were all dangerous fighters and looked unharmed, pissed off, but as fierce as ever. Seas claim anyone who got in their way.

I had thought seeing them fight was nerve-wracking before, but this was worse by far. Not being able to see them made me feel helpless, and from how tense Mel's shoulders were, I knew she was feeling the same.

I was surprised to hear Coral tell Mel, "She'll be okay. She might be a surface dweller, but she has the heart of siren."

I froze, ready to intervene and tell Coral that that wasn't a compliment, but to my surprise, Mel grinned. "She does, the heart of a warrior."

I was glad I had stayed quiet. It warmed my heart to see Coral smiling back at her.

After a few silent, tense minutes, a loud bang from the other ship captured our attention.

"What in the hells?" I cursed, grabbing both of the girls and pulling them closer before I saw what had caused the noise.

Scyla had come bursting out from belowdecks and had thrown one of the Saints into the main mast. The mast shook at the impact, but despite the loud noise, it didn't break. Mel cried out in relief when behind her came Tess carrying the missing siren in her arms, with Neta trailing right behind them.

Thank the seas they were all safe.

The others, both Daughters and Saints, flocked to them and I took a step toward their ship when I realized Tess was going to have to hold her own while holding the siren, too. Mel stepped in front of me, apparently having the same thought. I wasn't sure whether or not to stop her, but thankfully I didn't have to. The Daughters on the other ship surrounded Tess as they pulled into formation and fought their way step by step toward our ship.

Coral moved in between us and took both our hands. She didn't say anything, just squeezed us reassuringly as we watched the fight. I knew we all felt like we'd be more useful over there. If I didn't have them anchoring me here, I was sure I would be fighting too, and I knew Mel felt the same. Coral I couldn't be as sure about. Maybe she was having to hold herself back from jumping ship to be with her sisters, or maybe she wanted to help Tess and her recovered sister make it to freedom. I wasn't sure which urge would have been stronger, but I knew we were all fighting the same urge to help, and that helped me stay put.

They got closer to the railing and the Saints seemed to know they had lost. Their ship looked like it had suffered a call from the god of vengeance himself, and I was seas damned proud of us. There were always more Saints where these came from, but the Saints of Santerra would feel this loss.

The bodies littering their decks assured me that even if the ship managed to get away, the Saints would feel this defeat in their bones.

They deserved to rot.

As we watched, they pressed closer to the railing toward our ship.

"What's their plan?" I asked Mel.

Mel cocked her head in confusion before answering, "Tess is taking Rezi for a swim."

I was taken aback, but once I thought about it for more than a moment, I realized I was being foolish. That really was the only option. It wasn't like Tess was going to swing over here holding the siren.

They made it a little closer until the Saints in front of them were pressed against the railing. It didn't take much then, a wrong step from one, a botched dodge from another, and a few wild swings, and most of them were claimed by the sea, dragged to the depths by the sirens. That still left the Saints at their backs, but Tess and the siren were at the railing now.

I sucked in a breath as Tess looked over the edge, but the sea was clear now. The struggling Saints had been taken. The only thing alive in the depths right now were the sirens, which still, even after everything I had been through, I had to remind myself was a good thing. The sirens weren't going to hurt her.

Tess looked back up and said something to the siren, who nodded. She swung a leg over the rail. I marveled at her strength to be able to maneuver so easily while holding the siren. With her leg now planted on the ledge between the rail and open air, she swung her other leg over, bringing the siren with her.

I held my breath, but she glanced in our direction and grinned when she saw Mel, and with a wink, she stepped off the ledge. She and the siren plummeted into the water with a large splash.

Neta waited until Tess came up for air and waved to her to dive in after them.

I wondered what, if anything, the siren knew about Neta. Did she remember her sister at all? I hoped for her sake that her sister had been lucky enough to keep some of those memories. After all, it was possible, and they had known each other far longer than Cora and I had, so maybe there was still a part of her that recognized her sister. Neta surfaced a moment later, and we watched them swim the short distance to our boat.

Our crew tossed ropes out to the Daughters on the other ship, and they slowly started to retreat. Some of them quickly grabbed the ropes while others fended off the rest of the Saints. Surprising to no one, Scyla was still there fighting.

To our relief, the Daughters coming back  all appeared mostly fine. They were sore, bruised, and bloody, but they were alive and well enough to swing over, which was a blessing.

We were all relieved to see Tess and Neta come climbing back onto the ship. Mel dropped Coral's hand and raced over to them.

I took a step toward them and was surprised to see that Coral had already done the same but still hadn't dropped my hand. Together, we followed Mel.

Tess and Neta were soaked and dripping water all over the deck, but Mel was already in Tess's arms.

Tess had a goofy grin on her face as she held Mel tight. I was still watching her when we heard cries of alarm coming from the crew.

# Chapter Forty Nine
## Ray

We all ran toward the commotion. I dropped Coral's hand and palmed a dagger, trying to speed up so I was in front of her. We all pulled up short when we saw what the crew was yelling about.

It wasn't just the Daughters that had swung onto our ship. There was a Saint standing in the middle of their formed circle right across from Addie, who was glaring at him and holding him at sword point.

The Saint wasn't fighting back. He had his arms in the air and looked to be unarmed but he was staring at Addie like he had seen a ghost.

Addie's volume rose. "What in the seas are you doing here?" she yelled out.

The Saint's brows furrowed, and he pointed to his ears. A closer look showed they were plugged up. "I can't hear you," he said way louder than he needed to.

That didn't stop Addie from stepping closer and getting louder.

She was within his grasp now. I saw Tess tense, but she didn't make a move toward them yet.

If she trusted Addie's skills, I was going to have to, too.

Instead of changing tactics, Addie got louder. "What are you doing here?" she asked slowly, loudly.

Again, he shrugged and gestured to his ears. "I can't hear you. Is there somewhere more quiet?"

"Why don't you just take the plugs out?" she suggested with a mocking smile as she pressed the blade a little harder.

He leaned back a little, and I was surprised when Tess interjected, "Addie, is there a reason he's alive?"

Addie didn't turn to respond or take her eyes off him but spoke loud enough for us to hear. "I recognize him. He was on the ship the night we found Mel. He tried to help me. Not hard enough, but he tried."

Tess nodded, and I made a mental note to ask Addie about that later. A Saint had tried to help her? A Saint had tried to help a pirate? It had to be a story worth hearing and I couldn't believe she hadn't gotten around to telling it with all the drinking and sharing we had been doing.

"What?" he yelled out. "I'm not trying to hurt anyone."

Mel's laughter broke the tension and Tess chuckled a little despite herself before saying, "Get him belowdecks. He's useless up here, but make sure he's secure."

Addie led our new guest below deck with Neta following closely behind. I hoped we wouldn't regret it. I had been around the Saints long enough to have lost hope that there were any good ones. Even Cora's friends had turned on her.

"Does that mean we lost our room?" Coral asked me quietly.

I barked out a laugh before composing myself and saying, "Doubtful, he's probably in the real brig, not our cozy closet."

Coral looked startled, but before she could say anything else, there were shouts from the other ship. We all turned our attention to the other ship, and I was startled to see that Scyla was still over there fighting the Saints.

She wasn't the last one there, but she was close to it. Almost all of the other Daughters that were still alive had returned. Of course, she had to stay there until the last of them came back. If Tess hadn't rescued the siren herself, I was sure she would've done the same.

Scyla took her role as a protector of the Daughters quite seriously. I knew she was stalling, trying to buy time for any of the bodies of the fallen Daughters to show proof of life, but staying over there was foolish. If she didn't hurry up, she was going to end up joining them.

I itched to grab a rope and go help her, but I knew I would be more of a distraction to her than actual help, just another person she had to protect, so I stayed. Coral wrapped her hand around my arm. Whether to anchor herself or me, I wasn't sure.

Over the noises of the battle and the siren song below, we couldn't hear what Scyla was saying, but it was clear she was angry and looking to pile up more bodies.

When I saw her opponent, I understood why. She was going blade for blade with Captain Butcher. She was expertly wielding a short sword in each hand, but I wasn't sure if her skills would be enough.

Captain Butcher was ruthless. It was said that after he slaughtered the sirens, he would cut out their hearts and make a meal of them. He preached about the holiness of feasting on the devil before it could lay claim to you. Even when I thought the Sirens were the monsters, that practice sounded disgusting. Now, it was so much worse.

The sirens weren't monsters, and some of them weren't even strangers, but people's mothers, sisters, and daughters. He was succeeding in pressing her back. The bodies behind her were going to trip her up if she stepped much further.

"I have to help her," I said quietly.

Coral tensed. "You don't have to."

"I do."

"Please stay," she said, and the little quiver in her voice broke me. Coral's voice didn't shake or break. It was clear how scared she was, but she would be safe here, and I would never forgive myself if I didn't try to help Scyla. No one else had moved, but they didn't know Captain Butcher like I did. They trusted that Scyla was up to the challenge. I wasn't willing to let her bet her life on it. She had saved mine too many times for me to allow her to risk her own.

Coral tightened her hold on my arm before sighing and letting me go. I was getting to understand this siren version of the girl I loved. I took it as a good sign that she was worried for me and provided I survived the next few minutes, I hoped she would forgive me.

I turned to her and said, "Until the seas claim me, and even after, I will always find you," and pulled her closer. Her eyes widened, and I watched, staring into their swirling blue depths, looking for any sign of hesitation, giving her a chance to pull away. She didn't, so I pulled her lips to mine.

# CHAPTER FIFTY
# Ray

Her lips on mine felt electric. Kissing her as a siren already felt new and different, but it didn't compare to this. This kiss felt like coming home. My entire body tingled, and I never wanted the feeling to stop. In the back of my mind, I knew I was running out of time to get to Scyla.

With all the strength I had, I pulled away, knowing I had to move quickly before I changed my mind and stayed with her. She seemed in a daze and didn't acknowledge me when I told her softly, "Please forgive me."

I turned back to the other boat and saw Scyla wasn't looking good. She was backed into a corner and seemed determined to fight her way out of it instead of fleeing. She could've made it overboard if she tried, but she hadn't made a move to stop fighting Captain Butcher. Even from here, I could tell from the set of her face that this battle was to the death; hers or his. It wouldn't end until one of them dropped dead.

Tess had taken a step closer to the rail but hadn't yet shown any sign of joining Scyla. I eyed the ropes above us, calculating the angle I would need and took a couple of steps back. With my weight on the balls of my feet, I was ready to spring when I heard, "Ray?"

Coral's voice saying my name had tears welling in my eyes, but I steeled myself to ignore it. So what she had used my name for the first time instead of calling me her little huntress, I needed to help Scyla. Scyla hadn't faltered yet, but I was going to make sure she didn't.

I was poised to start again when I heard a sob coming from behind me. I couldn't stop myself from whipping around and saw Coral doubled over. I froze, not sure if I should run to her or keep going. Then she looked up and met my eyes and the pain in hers almost sent me to my knees.

"Ray," she choked out and through her tears, she was smiling. "You were right. Our love survived even after the seas claimed me."

That broke the last remaining shreds of composure. Somehow, by some miracle of the sea, she remembered me. Something about our kiss had brought back my Cora.

I could've kissed the Goddess herself for this blessing, but I couldn't make myself move. I was rooted to the spot.

Cora came to me slowly, like she didn't believe it either. She was almost to me when Tess screamed next to me.

Cora stopped, and we both looked at Tess. I had never heard Tess make a noise like that. I followed her eyes, already knowing what I would see, but needing to see it for myself. I faltered where I stood when I saw that I was too late to help Scyla. She had her back against the rail, but even with her back to us, I could see the steel that had been driven clean through her. Captain Butcher had her speared on his blade, straight through the heart. There was no surviving a wound like that.

He turned to us and grinned as he pulled the sword out of her and pushed her overboard.

I choked out a sob as she fell, knowing it was too late. I could go to her, but it was no use. That didn't stop Tess. In a flash of rope and steel, she touched down on their ship and took up the battle with the Butcher of the seas.

# Chapter Fifty One
# Coral

The memories were rushing around my mind, competing for my attention. I couldn't believe that my little huntress was *Ray*. I couldn't believe I had managed to forget her in the first place. Whatever happened when I transformed must have been powerful magic, because nothing short of that would have been enough to make me forget her.

The memories would have to wait, though, because Ray needed me. I couldn't make up for having forgotten her or for leaving her, but I could fix this. If I remembered right, the girl who just fell was her best friend here. I couldn't undo anything that had happened, but I knew I couldn't let her best friend die. There had to be something I could do. I didn't know if it would work, but I had to believe it would.

I knew this could be a huge mistake. I could lose myself to the siren again, but Ray had saved me once. I believed in her power to do it again.

I touched her shoulder lightly, knowing I would have to make the goodbye quick to get to her friend in time. The look of devastation on Ray's face left me feeling like I was the one who had been stabbed through the heart. I choked out, "I'm so sorry," hoping she would understand, and that she would forgive me eventually for what I was about to do.

I wasn't confident she had even heard me, but I hoped that some part of her would understand. She was the strongest woman I knew. She had sailed the seas for me, found me again, and saved me. Now I had to hope she was strong enough to forgive me.

I took a couple of quick steps back and then ran at the railing, vaulting over it and diving toward the sea. The last thing I heard before I hit the water was Ray screaming, "No!"

The water engulfed me, and when I opened my mouth, I was flooded with water and panic. My legs went numb, and I prayed to the seas that that was supposed to happen as I started trying to swim toward where I had seen the pirate fall.

Fighting my impulse to surface for air as I felt the weight of the water crushing my lungs, I fought my body, pushing forward, until suddenly, miraculously, the weight lifted and the water became as easy to breathe as the air had been. I pushed forward, kicking my feet, and shot forward. I looked back and was met with the welcome sight of purple scales.

My tail.

Thank the Goddess, because I was sure Ray would have killed me if I had drowned.

*Ray.*

I was a siren again–the tail made that clear–but miraculously I still had my memories.

My vision was better now, and I could see the girl's body. She was surrounded by my sisters.

*Charia,* I called out.

Her head snapped up and when her eyes met mine, I felt a jolt of pain at the volume of her voice in my head. *Coral! Nema bless you, you're back!*

I closed the gap, and they let me through. Ostoma was hard at work, trying to heal her.

*Is it working?* I asked.

Ostoma looked crestfallen when she answered, *I don't think we have a choice. There's nothing else to be done.*

We were running out of time. The girl's name came back to me in the cloud of memories. Scyla.

Ostoma took her hands off Scyla's chest and looked at Charia meaningfully. Charia was going to have to turn her.

Scyla was going to be a siren.

Hilarious, loud, bighearted Scyla, who I knew meant a lot to Ray, was going to be lost. Charia moved closer to her as the thought struck me. If I couldn't bring her back to Ray, at least I could be the one to save her. My sisters would take care of her and help her adjust. If she had to lose herself, at least there was a chance she could be found again.

*Let me,* I told Charia as I pressed forward.

She blinked in surprise. *Are you sure?*

I nodded. *It's my fault she's down here. I should be the one to help her.*

Ray had been going to help her, and I had stopped her. If I hadn't distracted her, Ray would've helped her, and things might not have ended up like this.

I couldn't fix what had been done, but I could save Scyla now.

*Tell me what to do,* I told Charia as I closed in on Scyla.

# Chapter Fifty Two
## Ray

An enraged Tess made quick work of killing Captain Butcher.

When he was dead, the rest of the Saints who still possessed a pulse dropped their weapons.

While Tess decided their fates, Mel held my hand as we watched the sea.

I was too far gone for hope. Scyla and Cora were both gone. Cora had remembered us and still decided to leave. She either sacrificed her memories trying to save Scyla, or she chose the sea over me. I should have known that her remembering was too good to be true. Mel and Tess knew everything there was to know about the sirens, but neither of them had ever mentioned anyone gaining their memories back after turning.

I was starting to question it myself. Everything had happened so quickly, maybe I had just heard what I wanted to hear.

"It's been too long," I said squeezing Mel's hand as the water stayed calm.

"There's still a chance," she said softly but I wasn't sure she even believed that herself. "At least we know Charia will tell us what happened. We won't have to wonder."

It was a small consolation, but it was a consolation regardless.

Tess came swinging back and we were all surprised to see that the remaining Saints were still alive. Normally that might have upset me, but with Cora lost again, I couldn't muster the energy to care about anything other than watching the sea.

"Anything?" Tess asked us.

I was grateful Mel answered since words weren't coming to me.

"Nothing yet, but if they don't come up themselves, Charia should be up shortly."

Mel and I kept our vigil, watching the seas while Tess ran around barking orders to the rest of the crew. I heard enough to get the gist that we weren't going to stay here for long. The Saints would come looking for their missing, and we didn't want to be here when they found the casualties. It made sense, but there was nothing rational to me about leaving Cora again.

Granted, she could already be miles away from here. I was sure she was a fast swimmer. There was a chance she wasn't even still down there, but I couldn't stop watching.

When the surface broke, I expected to see Charia's white hair and grey tail, but instead, I saw dark locs and warm brown skin. I held my breath, not trusting my eyes, but Mel's tight squeeze on my hand told me she saw her too. Scyla was still breathing. The water next to her rippled and I audibly gasped when I saw Cora's dark hair come into view. I knew in my heart it was her without even seeing her face. Charia surfaced right after her.

The others started to cheer. It was then that Cora looked up and waved at me, and my strength broke. I started sobbing. She wasn't lost to me after all. Whatever version of her this was, Cora or Coral, she had come back to me.

As they swam closer though, it became clear that something wasn't right. Scyla was angry. From the way they were flanking her, if I didn't know better, I would have said it looked like Charia and Cora were dragging her to us.

Something wasn't right, and then I saw what I had managed to miss before. Under the water, where there should have been Charia's grey tail and Cora's purple tail, there was also a dark teal tail that almost blended in with the water.

Scyla's legs were nowhere to be seen.

The cheers died out as the others saw what I was seeing. When they got closer, it was clear Scyla was thrashing in their hold, trying to escape them, to get away from us. It was heartbreaking to watch.

Scyla, at least the version we knew, hadn't made it after all.

We lowered a lifeboat and they had to drag her into it with them. Before they had even made it to the deck, we all knew she wouldn't be staying.

Charia was the first to speak. "We didn't get to her in time."

"Scyl," Tess said, taking a step toward the boat, but Mel grabbed her arm, keeping her in place.

At the same time, Scyla bared her now dangerously sharp teeth at us.

"She's not herself," Mel said carefully.

Cora spoke up now. "She doesn't remember anything. She was dying, and I had to turn her. I'm so sorry."

"You did everything you could," Tess was quick to say, and I was incredibly grateful.

"She'll be coming back with me," Charia said. "I had hoped that seeing you all might jog something in her mind. It was foolish, but with Coral remembering, I thought it was worth a shot."

I was the worst sort of friend because Scyla was lost to us, and I was having trouble thinking past the fact that the siren said Cora remem-bered.

Cora looked at me then and said, "I remember everything. I'd like to stay... if you'll have me."

"You're my north star. Of course I'll have you. The seas know how hard I've been trying to find you."

She grinned at that and looked at Tess who had a soft smile.

"You're both welcome as long as you'd like." Tess turned back to Charia and said, "Promise me you'll take good care of her."

Charia nodded. "I'll care for her like my own. She's one of us now."

Mel squeezed Tess's shoulder reassuringly and said to Charia, "I'm glad you're here. Thank you for saving her."

The emotions were tumbling around inside me. I was elated and devastated. The seas had brought Cora back to me, just to take away Scyla. Cora had come back to me though. I had to believe that somehow we could find a way to bring Scyla back too.

"Is there anything we can do for her?" I asked, not willing to hope but needing to ask.

Charia hesitated. "To tell you the truth, I don't know. Before Coral, I would've said no, but she tells us she remembers everything, so I can't rule out the same possibility for Scyla."

"We know you'll do everything you can for her," Mel said.

Charia nodded, and Tess added, "Please do whatever you can to bring our girl home."

"By the seas and Nema herself, I swear it."

There was nothing more to be said, and sensing that, Cora pulled herself out of their boat and landed with a thud on the deck. I hadn't moved to help her until that point, not wanting to get closer to Scyla and scare her, but I couldn't stop myself then.

I rushed over to Cora and knelt down next to her, pulling her into my arms. I held her close as the others lowered Charia and Scyla back into the water.

As good as it felt having Cora back in my arms again, a part of my heart was breaking seeing Scyla go. Seeing her eyes had changed from their warm brown to the eerie swirling blue, seeing her go from so alive and so human one minute to a siren in the worst sense of the word the next minute, was too much to process.

We watched them in silence until Charia and Scyla disappeared under the water.

"I didn't know her as well as you did, but I'm so sorry, Ray," Cora said quietly.

Her voice, her calling me by my name, were comfort I hadn't imagined I would ever have again, and it soothed part of the ache.

"You would have loved her," I said with a smile. "She's fierce, strong, ridiculously loyal, as optimistic as you, and down for pretty much any bad idea."

Cora laughed. "From what I saw of her, I already know I would have loved her. Not that it was a high bar for me though. I love every one of these pirates for what they did for you. They took care of you when I couldn't, and they helped you find your way back to me."

I couldn't help the tears that started to fall. "And the sirens did that for you?"

"They did. They got me through the worst day of my life, the day that should have been my last. They saved me and helped me find myself."

"But you're okay with leaving them?"

"For you? No question. You're my home. Besides, I just proved I can go visit them whenever I want now that I know I can transform without losing myself."

"It was a big risk," I said.

"I know how much Scyla means to you, I wasn't going to let you lose her."

"I could've lost you again though," I protested.

"And if you had, I'm sure you would've found a way back into my heart again. Siren or not, it'll always be yours."

She reached up to brush away my tears, but her hand fell on her locket.

"My locket!" she squealed. "You found it? I thought it was lost."

"Garrick had it, so I stabbed him and stole it back."

She grinned. "I hope you made it hurt."

I laughed. That was the last thing I expected her to say. "I did."

She reached around my neck, pausing a moment and asking, "Can I?"

"Of course, it's yours."

She smiled at that, unclasping the necklace and pulling it toward her.

"How about we get you settled, and I'll help you put it on?"

"Thank you," she said, leaning toward me. I met her halfway, kissing her. Her lips tasted of the sea but I devoured her like only she could parch my thirst.

I heard Mel call out, "Why don't you take that belowdecks?"

I pulled away from Cora immediately and looked over at Mel who shrugged. "Someone's gotta do the heckling while Scyla's away."

A few more bittersweet tears fell at that. Cora reached up again and gently brushed them away with a little laugh saying, "Hey, I thought we were trying to get me dry."

I looked down at her surprised. "You want to transform back? I thought you'd want to go back to your tub."

"I've had enough of the water for today, actually."

That was all I needed to hear. I scooped her up, holding her tight to my chest and carried her below deck to find her some clothes and a more permanent place to stay.

# Chapter Fifty Three
## Ray

She insisted on spending the night in my hammock with me. Tess gave her one of her own, of course, but she was adamant she had already spent too much time away from me.

It was a bit of a tight squeeze, but I wasn't complaining about having her in my arms.

I held her, waiting for sleep to claim me, but it didn't. It was hard to ignore the silence coming from where Scyla would normally be.

I knew I was mourning her more than I should be, especially when she was still alive. Some Daughters had actually lost their lives today and while I mourned for them, I was mourning for Scyla more.

The guilt was eating at me.

I could tell from Cora's breathing that she wasn't any closer to sleep than I was.

I was about to suggest a stroll on the deck when I heard a whisper. "You guys up?"

The room was pitch black, but I didn't need light to know it was Addie.

"Yeah," Cora answered for us.

"Wanna come have a drink with me?"

I looked down at Cora, who nodded and lifted her head from its resting spot on my chest. The movement unbalanced the hammock, and we started to wobble.

I held the sides attempting to steady it, laughing at Cora's scowl. "Just give us a second to get untangled," I said to Addie. "You get used to it," I told Cora.

She managed to disentangle herself and get her feet on the floor. "I never thought I'd be willing sleep in a net," she huffed out, making Addie and me laugh.

I pulled myself out, took Cora's hand and we followed Addie. "Anyone else coming?"

"Just the usual suspects," she said quietly as we walked by some of the others. "Us, Tess, Mel, and Neta."

It was hard to hear the usual suspect not include Scyla, but being with the others tonight, mourning her absence and the losses of the other Daughters who didn't make it back, might help to quiet the ache in my chest.

I wondered how Addie was taking it. She and Scyla had been close too, practically thick as thieves. She hadn't been there when it happened, and I don't know if that made things any better or worse for her. Even being there, I had felt helpless. I suspected Addie's absence had made her feel even more helpless, having no idea what was even happening as she brought the Saint belowdecks.

"What happened with our new guest anyway?" I asked.

Addie's quick steps faltered a moment before she said, "He's not drinking with us if that's what you're asking."

I snorted out a laugh. "Of course that's not what I'm asking."

"He's in the brig for now until we decide what to do with him."

I was going to ask more but then we arrived at Tess's door.

Addie opened it without knocking. Tess was sprawled out on the floor with Mel on her lap. Neta was standing by the porthole watching the horizon.

"Addie's back!" Mel said with a hiccup.

Tess smiled up at us, and gestured to Mel. "She couldn't make it to a chair."

"I so could have, you're just comfier," Mel said with a huff.

Cora squeezed my hand, and I looked over to see her smiling at the pair. I squeezed hers back.

I didn't know what our future looked like, what Cora would want it to look like, but I knew that I would find a way to shape it however she wanted. If Tess and Mel could make their relationship work as a siren and a pirate, I was sure we could do the same. Cora was my own little miracle, and I was going to keep her as long as she would let me.

Addie flopped onto the floor next to them and elbowed Mel saying, "You did save me some didn't you?"

Tess laughed. "*I* did. I had to cut her off at some point." She gave Mel a pointed look and said, "Some people aren't built to drink like a fish."

"Hey!" Mel said quickly while I tried not to laugh. "As one of the only two fish here, I'm entitled to drink however much I want. Spicy or not, water's my domain."

We all laughed at that, and Cora and I settled on the floor across from the others. "Want some spicy water?" Tess asked passing the bottle to me with a chuckle. I took a deep swig that burned like cannon fire going down. I offered it to Cora, but she shook her head, so I passed it back to Tess.

We stayed like that for a while, enjoying each other's company. I knew they were feeling the way I was even if it wasn't quite the same for all of us. We all missed Scyla and the other lost Daughters, and knowing we were hurting together made it a little easier to bear.

After a little while, Neta surprised us all by drifting over, grabbing the bottle from Tess, and saying, "If you're expecting me to be the life of the party, Goddess help us all."

The tension broke with our laughter.

"That would be a sight Scyla would come crawling out of the sea for," Tess said, laughing.

"By the time she gets back, she's going to want to kill all of us for everything she missed out on," I said. There was nothing Scyla hated more than being left out of something, good or bad, she always wanted to be included.

"You know," Addie said in a more serious tone, "I think I'll start keeping records of the things she missed for her. When she comes back, I don't want her to feel like she missed out on everything."

"That's not a bad idea," Tess said, smiling.

"We could write her letters too," I suggested, and Addie's smile grew.

"She'd love that!"

"That'd be a great way to help ease her back in when she returns. It'll show her how loved and missed she was," Cora said.

"You think it'll take long?" I asked.

"Knowing Charia, I doubt it," Cora said reassuringly.

"She'll make Nema herself fix it," Mel said confidently.

"You think she'll help?" Tess asked.

"Goddess or not, when Charia wants something, you don't wanna be on her bad side. If Nema knows what's good for, her she'll help."

It was good to hear that, and it noticeably lightened the mood. We had a little more to drink, toasting to Scyla and her bravery and wishing her safety and a quick return, then toasting to the rest of the Daughters we lost today, wishing them peace.

As the night wound back into morning, we shared our favorite stories about Scyla. It was comforting to know that even in the tough times, the Daughters were there for each other, that we took care of each other. It was even more comforting to know that Cora and I would always have a place with them for as long as we wanted it.

Cora was and would always be my home, but losing her brought me something else I'd never had: a family. For the first time in my life, I felt like I belonged somewhere, and I wouldn't be quick to give this up.

I had never thought about the after. I had been so focused on finding Cora that I never really stopped to think about what we would do or where we would go once I got her back.

We had the world at our feet now. We could go pretty much anywhere and do pretty much anything. Of course, I couldn't imagine leaving before Scyla came back, but the seas had returned Cora to me, so I knew Scyla would be back one day, too. It was just a matter of time.

One thing was for certain: whatever the future held, Cora and I would face every adventure together.

# EPILOGUE
# Coral

-A Month Later-

"Are you sure you want to do this?" I asked Ray for what was probably the hundredth time. "I know I got mine changed, but you don't have to. You could get it removed if you wanted."

I was worried that she was doing this just to make me happy, and that was the last thing I wanted. I didn't need her to alter herself in any way for me. I loved her for her, and even losing my memory hadn't been enough to change that. She had to know she didn't have to do this for me.

She shook her head. "It's a part of me and a part of our story. You couldn't pay me to remove it, but I'm all for improving it."

"Are you sure?" I asked again. "You could get anything you want."

Just because I had followed the Daughters' lead and added a siren to my anchor didn't mean she had to do it too. For me, it was the symbol of the Daughters but also a nod to my time with my sisters. I don't know if I considered myself human again or if I was more of a land siren like Mel, but it didn't change the fact that having been a siren was a part of my story. Thinking about it, it made sense that Ray would feel the same about being a Daughter.

"I know, and this is what I want."

Ray looked over at Flora and nodded to her.

"Ready?" Flora asked.

"Definitely," Ray said grinning.

Flora went in with her needles and the image started to change. First the tail came into view, wrapped around the anchor. When the tail gained its color, I gasped.

Instead of the green that the Daughters normally used, the tail was a violet purple, like my own tail was, like my tattoo was.

"It's me," I breathed out.

Ray smiled up at me from where she was sitting. "Of course it is. Did you think I'd get some other siren tattooed on me?"

I laughed at that, and Flora had to tell Ray not to move since it would mess up her work.

We stayed quiet after that, but watching myself be etched permanently on Ray's skin nearly moved me to tears. Flora's art was beautiful, second only to Ray's own art.

"Do you think you could teach me?" Ray asked quietly.

I held my breath, not wanting to do or say anything to influence Flora's answer or change Ray's mind. As far as I knew, Ray hadn't drawn anything since she left the Convent. We had both been healing and rebuilding our lives together, but as much as she seemed to be improving, she hadn't picked her art back up.

I didn't think she would until Scyla came back.

I had thought about suggesting she work with Flora, but I hadn't wanted to push. She and I had been dragged through the hells and back, and if she didn't feel like making art anymore, it would have been a loss to the world, but I wouldn't have blamed her. "I'd love to!" Flora said quickly. "A lot of the basics are the same as drawing. Are you any good at drawing?"

"She's the best!" I rushed to say.

Ray blushed, saying, "I'm alright, I'm not that great."

"Don't listen to her," I told Flora, then turned back to Ray and said, "You're amazing at everything you do, but drawing is one of the things you excel at."

To my delight, she started training with Flora soon after. Seeing her working on her art again that first time brought tears to my eyes. So much had changed for her, for us both, and I was overjoyed she didn't let go of that part of herself.

Ray was feeling guilty about not spending as much time with me, but between Mel and Addie, they made sure I stayed busy and felt welcome. Neta even started combat training me, sparring with me every day. Tess would help out when she was free, too. Everyone was really making an effort to make me feel like I belonged here, and it was working.

Sparring and life on the ship in general were grueling and hard work, but it was worth it. Ray worried I was just staying here for her, but I loved the ship too. I loved the Daughters that I now claimed as my sisters, and loved that they were trying to protect my other sisters–the sirens.

As long as the sirens were in danger, I couldn't see myself living any-where else or doing anything different.

It was hard to deny that I did miss my sisters though. There was technically nothing stopping me from visiting them, from going and checking on Scyla, Charia, and the others, but I didn't feel like I could leave Ray. She was destroyed when we were separated, and I didn't want her to have to worry and miss me again.

When Mel came to me with a proposition though, I wasn't sure how to say no.

"You–" I faltered, trying to find the words. I couldn't believe what she was asking. "You want to transform?"

She sighed. "I don't know if I want to, but I think I should. I've been hiding from that part of myself for too long and it's about time I faced it."

"You don't have to. You know you don't have anything to prove right?"

"Says the girl who called me a land siren," she said pointedly.

"I didn't mean–"

She waved me off with a sigh. "You're not wrong though. I bet that's what our sisters think of me, that I'm a surface-dweller now."

"I swear on the seas they love you. They miss you, and I doubt they understand your choice, but they still love you. On land or not, you have the heart of a siren and no one can take that from you."

"I know, I know. I know no one else looks at me like an outsider but it's hard not to feel that way when I'm pulled between two worlds. You must get it."

I did. It was different for me since I started as a human though. Mel was Mer before she became a siren. We came from different worlds and yet we were both here, torn between the two, both fish out of water.

"I do."

"I know. You might be the only one who does, so I know you'll understand when I say that it's time I faced my fears and went for a swim. With you here, I'm not in any danger of losing myself. I trust you."

I knew how much of an honor that was, and I didn't take it lightly, but I had to ask, "Why now?"

"Because Scyla's out there. If there's anything we can do to help bring her home, I'd face every single one of my fears to do it."

I felt the same, so we told Ray and Tess together. It was clear neither of them loved the idea, but neither was willing to shut down anything that could help Scyla.

Addie had the idea to start small and have Mel transform for the first time in my old tub. With Tess and I standing by, she did, and nothing terrible happened. She still was very much herself, just with a bright blue tail.

After a few days, we worked up to swimming laps around the boat. After that, it was clear Tess and Mel were both feeling much more comfortable. I was too. Getting to swim around with Mel, getting to be a siren without having to worry about being a danger to others, was exhilarating.

We promised Ray and Tess we wouldn't be gone long and assured them we'd look out for each other.

None of us had voiced it, but we had expected Charia to check in with us and let us know how Scyla was doing. We weren't sure if no news was good news, and Mel was right; it was past time we went to pay them a visit and find out for ourselves. I missed my sisters, and whether or not she knew it, Scyla needed us.

Scyla was a Daughter of the Deep and no amount of siren instincts could change that. Between Mel and me, I was sure we would find a way to get her back. If it took longer, we could keep visiting until she was ready, but whatever it took, Goddess willing, we would bring her home.

# More Santerran Sea Stories

Want more of the Daughters of the Deep?

Check out the prequel novella

*A High Seas Heist*

On the Isles of Santerra...

The all female pirate crew, the Daughters of the Deep, are the only thing standing between the Saints of Santerra and their goal of slaughtering every siren in the sea.

The rest of the Isles of Santerra believe in the mission of the Saints, but the Daughters know that the real monsters aren't the sirens, but the Saints who seek to slaughter them.

The Daughters won't rest until the seas are safe from the Saints.


And coming soon...
Stay tuned for Scyla's story

# ABOUT THE AUTHOR

 Sarah Zane is an author of happy endings for traumatized queers.

As a bisexual, it should be shocking to no one that she has more than one genre she loves and writes. She writes across genres but guarantees that a Sarah Zane book will always be queer and always have a happy ending eventually. She has a particular fondness for writing sapphic pairings since they tend to be underrepresented in books.

She lives in New England with her 2 black cats named Gatsby and Mr. Darcy. When she isn't writing, she can be usually be found taking forest walks, visiting castles, planning exotic trips she can't afford, or cuddled up with one of her cats crying over fictional characters or yelling at them about how badly they need therapy.

For more from Sarah Zane, check out...

*The Beautiful Fools Duet*
*Beautiful Little Fool – Book One*
*An Illusion Shattered – Book Two*
*A sapphic, feminist retelling of the Great Gatsby from Daisy's POV.*

### *Off Script: A Book Ball Fantasy Adventure*

*A fantasy adventure story about Sadie, a fantasy author whose first convention goes haywire when her characters literally jump off the page.*

### *Cosplay and Confrontation*

*A sapphic rivals-to-lovers cosplayers romcom that takes place at the same fantasy convention in Off Script.*

### *Under Lock and Key*

*A sapphic cozy fantasy retelling of Bluebeard about a blue-haired temptress innkeeper and the mysterious woman who wanders into her inn and falls for her charms.*

### *Becoming A Bi-con*

*A sapphic spicy rivals-to-lovers fake dating popstar romance about Savannah Hollywood and her ex-best friend/old costar Maya Ryder.*

# Acknowledgements

There are so many people responsible for getting me and this book to where it is today, but I can't write the acknowledgements without mentioning how hard this book was to write. This book is the one that's been plaguing me for years, the first one I wanted to write and the one I was sure I was never going to be good enough to do justice to. I'm incredibly proud of myself and happy to say that I wrote the story I set out to fifteen years ago when the idea first came to me. Thank you to everyone who pushed me to keep going and to write this story, it means the world to me that it's out there in the world and that it's the story teenage me would have been proud of.

To C, who snuck your way into this book and who's character ended up demanding another book, you changed this book and my life for the better.

To Willow who gave me the much needed pep talk that ensured this book stayed on track.

To my East Coast Baddies aka the East Coast Author Alliance aka the East Coast Bitches aka Willow and Grace, thank you guys for the much needed motivational sprints and writing sessions that are always just as productive as they are fun.

To my family and friends, thank you as always for continuing to support me.

Last but never least, thank you to you dear reader for supporting me and my books.

From the bottom of my heart, I love you all.